An Assumption of Death

AN ASSUMPTION OF DEATH

Roy Lewis

Constable · London

First published in Great Britain 2000
by Constable & Company Ltd
3 The Lanchesters, 162 Fulham Palace Road
London W6 9ER

Copyright © 2000 Roy Lewis

The right of Roy Lewis to be identified as the author of
this work has been asserted by him in accordance with
the Copyright, Designs and Patents Act 1988

ISBN 0 094 80280 7

Typeset in Palatino 10pt by Photoprint, Torquay, Devon
Printed and bound in Great Britain by MPG Books Ltd,
Bodmin, Cornwall

A CIP catalogue record for this book is available from the
British Library

'I heard the cry of an eagle, loud above the voices of many other birds. It seemed to say, "We have been waiting for you. We knew you would come ... You will have a ghost with you always – another self."' Lame Deer, of the Lakota Sioux.

PROLOGUE

The Spanish fishing boat lifted idly in a long, slow swell. The Yorkshire coastline was a hazy, distant line, shimmering in the warm sunshine of the Indian summer the north had been experiencing. The skipper of the boat maintained a sullen silence as the nets were dragged in under the watchful eyes of the British customs officers.

Two were already down below, sweating in their search for the drug haul, following the anonymous tip-off received thirteen hours earlier. So far it looked as though the search was going to be unproductive. It was possible that the trawler skipper himself had received a warning and got rid of anything he might have had on board. Or the tip-off itself had been wrong – or malicious. Such things happened.

Alderson, the leader of the boarding party, was fresh-faced, looked younger than his years but was experienced enough. He had an odd feeling about this case. The trawler had been shadowed out of its Spanish home base, tracked until it entered British waters and identified as fishing illegally. It was why now he was not hopeful of finding what they were looking for. A fishing boat on a drug run was unlikely to draw attention to itself by fishing illegally off the North Yorkshire coast.

One of the two officers came up from down below and caught the leader's eye. He shook his head glumly. The machinery clanked as the net was wound in, and seagulls wheeled above their heads, screaming in anticipation at the likely harvest. Suddenly there was a screeching of metal as the winding gear seemed to snag, and the Spanish skipper snarled. 'Madre de dios!' He cast a furious glance in the direction of the customs officers as though the fault lay with them and dashed towards the side, leaning over the gunwale to stare down at the nets. Silver flashes came from the struggling fish caught in the twisted toils but he ignored them, staring downwards to see what had happened to snag the straining nets.

7

'What's up?' asked the junior customs officer.

Alderson shrugged. 'Something dragging at the nets. I've got a bad feeling about this one. I don't think we're going to find anything. It's a wild-goose chase. You think we've been conned – getting our attention diverted so some other boat can slip inshore?'

'Could be.'

Alderson lifted his glance to peer towards the hazy shoreline. They had been informed that a possible landing would be attempted at dusk, somewhere off Staithes, or Robin Hood's Bay. It had always seemed a bit odd to him – Robin Hood's Bay might claim a romantic connection with the legendary outlaw but it was not exactly a place where he would have expected a drug run to terminate. Teesport now, that was different – there was an active drug run into Middlesbrough and had been for years. But this . . . he suspected this whole thing was just a hoax. However, they had to check. Behind him the Spanish skipper was shouting furious imprecations. Then, oddly, there was a shocked silence. Alderson turned his glance away from the shoreline to look at the Spanish skipper. He was leaning over the side, his hands gripping the gunwale. His body was stiff with shock.

Alderson moved forward to stand by his side. He peered over. He saw then what had snagged the nets. There was something tangled in the net, something heavy and dark, lifting slowly in the water, and close to the propellers at the rear of the boat. He leaned out further to stare at it. The Spanish skipper crossed himself. The heavy, sodden bundle seemed shapeless, but there was no mistaking the maimed hand that drifted listlessly near the surface.

'Hell's flames!'

It took them almost an hour to disentangle the corpse and haul it on deck. Two of the fishermen, hardened though they were, vomited as the corpse came on board. One refused to come near it, crossing himself and muttering in Catalan. Alderson himself felt his stomach churning as he supervised the activity. When the corpse lay there they could see that the fishes had fed well on what had once been a man. The body had been fully clothed when it went in, but part of the clothing had been lost. One hand was completely missing, while the other lacked fingers, apparently nibbled away during the immersion. But what turned their stomachs was the fact that the corpse lacked a head. The neck had been gashed deeply, its pale white flesh eaten away. The body was still clad in trousers but the shoes had disappeared and the feet had also suffered from the depredations of the fish. There was a strong, malodorous smell in the air as Alderson radioed in to base.

He glanced at the Spanish skipper, whose weatherbeaten face was white under his dirty tan. 'You know anything about this?' Alderson realised the question was foolish even as he asked it.

The Spaniard stared at him vacantly. '*No es mi problema, aquí. Soy marinero, solamente. Este hombre . . . yo no sé, yo no sé.*'

He didn't know him; didn't know anything about the corpse that had been snagged in their nets, the body that might have been decapitated by his propellers. And with no head and no hands to work on, Alderson guessed, forensic scientists would have difficulty establishing an identity.

'Hey, look at this, sir!'

One of the customs officers, whose curiosity was as strong as his stomach, was kneeling beside the corpse, peering at the chest, gingerly lifting what was left of the tattered shirt.

'What is it?' Alderson asked, his gorge rising.

'He was wearing a money belt when he went in, sir. It's still strapped to him, under the remains of his shirt.'

Perhaps the forensic scientists would have something to work on after all, Alderson thought to himself as he began to explain, with gestures, that he was insisting that the Spanish boat turned in to head for Whitby. He wanted no more to do with this – there were others better qualified to handle it.

The Spanish skipper was of the same opinion. Within minutes of the nets being hauled in the boat was headed for the North Yorkshire coast, and the haven of Whitby.

PART ONE

1

At dawn, the rising sun sent long fingers of gold slipping along the red cliff edges, and the desert seemed to glitter as sharp glances of light gleamed from shards of mica and quartz in the striated rock. The temperature rose swiftly from the bitter cold of the night and small whirling dust devils danced at the foot of the cliff the way they had danced for a thousand years. It was a mystical time, the deep silence of the land denying that men had lived here for millennia, now that it was all returned to dust, and desiccation and death.

The ancient stone houses that had been carved into the cliff face gaped mutely at the small group on the ridge: eroded by time and the sand storms that regularly scoured them, they looked out on an empty, dead landscape. The desert wind had carved wider the apertures that had let in light; the old stone steps had crumbled and collapsed over time and sand had half buried the ruins, but the harsh, bright light about them was as brilliant as ever and in this magical time between darkness and dawn there was a tension, a sense of excitement as the rosy half light gave way to the sharp, piercing brightness that picked out with long shadows the works that had been left by man.

'It's the best moment to see the site, for the first time,' Professor Schwartz suggested. 'You can see the whole area highlighted – a clear distinction between light and darkness that seems to pick out the main features . . . the cliff dwellings themselves, the corral over there for the beasts, the lines of ancient walls where they practised their primitive agriculture. Later in the day, as the sun gets high in the sky and the heat is more intense, it's not so easy to pick out the main points.'

'It's such a beautiful time,' Jane Wilson breathed. Don Schwartz smiled, glancing at her indulgently. In his mid-forties, he was a big man, well over six feet in height, broad-shouldered, craggy-featured, dressed in denim jacket, worn jeans and desert boots. He towered over her small frame, but he treated her almost delicately, as though she were his daughter, with a care and pleasure that belied his usual rugged manner and direct speech. Arnold guessed Don Schwartz was very fond of Jane but perhaps had not yet come to terms with, or properly analysed, his feelings towards her.

'Corrals?' Arnold said. 'But horses weren't introduced until the time of the Spanish conquest.'

'Of course,' Schwartz agreed, flicking a dark-eyed glance in his direction. 'And *corral* comes from the Spanish tongue. But it's a good enough word to use for animal pens, even if these people didn't use it.' His tone became quizzical. 'You a semantic expert, Mr Landon?'

'Hardly.'

'But pernickety. Precise. English. That's good in an archae-ologist. Cuts down on the mistakes.' Professor Schwartz grunted. 'Anyway, let's go take a closer look at the site, and where we've been excavating over the years. Better now than in the heat of the day.'

Arnold and Jane followed Don Schwartz as he made his way down the hill, scrambling through low brush, away from the ridge where they had camped, into the valley and across towards the cave dwellings on the far hillside. Arnold had been in the States for five days now, at Jane Wilson's invitation. She had suggested that he take a holiday with her, join her in her expedition to the Mojave desert where she had wangled an invitation to visit a site of historic interest. He had flown to New York, where she now lived, and together they had made the long flight across the States to Los Angeles, where they had been met by Professor Schwartz, of the University of New Mexico.

'I met him at a conference six months ago,' Jane had explained. 'It turned out he was familiar with my historical novels – light reading after a long day's work – and we became friendly. He more than half persuaded me I ought to write something about early America. So when he invited me to the site he's working on in the Mojave desert I immediately thought of you. I'd been talking of coming back to England, but things are difficult and I've been far too busy so this seemed a great opportunity for us to get together again – and I knew you'd love to poke around these old ruins.'

14

Arnold had had some leave due to him; it had not been too difficult to arrange two weeks off and so he had booked his tickets, joined her, and now he was enjoying himself enormously.

They spent the morning wandering through the ancient cave dwellings where Don Schwartz pointed out the main features of the excavations. There had been a pause in the work recently, but it was due to begin again in a week's time and Schwartz, in charge of the project, was making a preliminary visit to set things in order. He had seemed a little reserved when Jane had first introduced him but when Arnold's interest became apparent he had warmed and become more enthusiastic. Nevertheless, Arnold suspected that Schwartz would have preferred showing the site to Jane alone, rather than with a male companion.

She had changed, in a subtle way. When Arnold had met her first, some years ago, he had thought her plain. Later, as their relationship developed, he had come to appreciate more the way her features could change, light up, so that there were times when he thought her almost beautiful. But since she had come to the States she seemed to have matured, gained in confidence, and the book successes and the film deal that her agent had struck for her had brought her into a new world where she had been flattered, wined, dined, lionised . . . it had lifted her, given her greater poise. He could understand why Don Schwartz was attracted.

'Much of the work we're doing is a replication of what's already been done elsewhere in the south-west.' Don Schwartz's voice boomed in the narrow confines of the dim cave dwelling. 'We've been able to confirm many theories that had been extrapolated from other sites, but the big excitement here is that we've found something that we regard as unique. Follow me through here . . .'

It was a narrow entrance, carved in the rock. It led into a low, narrow passage: Schwartz was forced to bend low as he led the way. The beam of his torch illuminated the tunnel well enough because of its narrowness, but eventually they emerged into a wider area, a chamber some eight feet high, chiselled out of the living rock, which the torch lit only dimly as its light glanced off the walls, ancient dust dancing and drifting in its beam.

15

'What *is* this?' Jane asked, looking about her.

'We discovered it about four years ago,' Schwartz explained eagerly. 'There'd been a rock fall at the entrance which had kept it hidden for centuries – we've found no evidence of human usage here for at least five hundred years, anyway. As for the chamber itself, we've interpreted it as a holy site, a place of worship and of burial. We found only three skeletons in here. They were of different generations and our guess is that they were the remains of holy men. But we also found this . . .'

His torch beam wavered, seeking, then flashed against the far wall. Arnold stepped closer, peering in the dimness, squinting at the area covered by the bright torchlight. At a height of about six feet there were indentations, carvings in the rock. He stared at them, tracing the outlines. 'I can't quite make out . . .'

Don Schwartz moved to stand beside him and leaned forward, running a stubby, rough-skinned finger along the lines of the carving. 'You see here . . . a depiction of a house, almost childlike . . . then this symbolic drawing which we've interpreted as the universe, with its four sides representing the cardinal directions. This post here, we think it represents the cosmic tree breaking through the levels of the cosmos –'

Arnold grimaced. 'That seems somewhat –'

'We have an iconography that supports the interpretation,' Schwartz said drily, recognising the doubt in Arnold's tone. 'But more interesting is this section here. You see what it represents?'

Arnold stared at it in the unwavering beam of the torchlight. Jane was close beside him, leaning slightly against him, one hand on his shoulder. 'I'm not sure . . . It appears to be a man, but he has wings, and he seems to be flying . . .'

'And this?'

Arnold studied the carving carefully for a long while. It was Jane who finally recognised it for what it was. 'The head of a man. His mouth open. Another smaller figure emerging from his mouth –'

'That's right,' Schwartz interrupted eagerly, jabbing with his finger at the carvings. 'And this is a world tree again, or pillar; this the Milky Way; the upper world, the lower world, a flying figure, a spirit soul. And this circle here, we think it represents a *tinguna.*'

'A what?'

'*Tinguna* . . . a kind of electromagnetic force field is the best way to describe it.' Schwartz grunted his pleasure, displaying the kind of excitement that would have been his when the carvings were first discovered. 'Isn't it stupendous?'

'The carvings are indeed a real find. Have you dated them?' Arnold asked.

'We think maybe seven hundred years. But more than that is the fact that none of this should be here.'

'I don't understand,' Arnold said, touching the carvings lightly with his fingers.

'This is clearly a holy place, one used to inter revered, power-ful men in the tribe. But it shouldn't be here, because we've found nothing previously in the south-west area to match it.'

'No other carvings, you mean?'

'No other *shamanistic* carvings, or paintings. We're talking here of spirit souls emerging from the mouth, of shamanistic flight, a soaring, a roaming through the stars.'

'And there's nothing else like this in any of the sites in the Mojave desert?'

Don Schwartz shook his head, and turned, leading them back out of the chamber, through the tunnel into the cave room beyond. He switched off his torch, leaned in the aperture that formed a window and looked out across the dry, dusty valley, his eyes slitted against the glare, harsh against the dimness of the cave dwelling interior. 'No,' he said, 'nothing. We've plenty of evidence at the other sites of visions, occasional paintings of initiation ceremonies, sweat-lodges, medicine men . . . but generally in this region we don't see representations of shamanic soul-flight – they tend to occur mainly in the Arctic and sub-Arctic cultures. And the north-west coast is culturally very var-ied so there's a tendency for some trance and spirit-journeying to be found at Salish and as far south maybe as Yurok, but around here . . .'

He turned to glance at Arnold. 'The north is different. Among the Esquimaux peoples shamans functioned much as they did in northern Siberia. Here in the south-west of the States all the

17

evidence has been that, rather than undergo the Siberian experience of involuntary torture and dismemberment by the spirits, shamans sought initiation through isolation and fasting. The role of trance and journeying was taken by dreaming, or by a vision quest – going into the wilderness, fasting for days, to obtain a vision of the spirit.'

'The Plains Indians did that sort of thing, I believe,' Jane said. 'Young men were encouraged to go out into the desert, to seek the Manitou.'

Schwartz nodded. 'That's right. And that's why this site is of great importance and significance. It seems as though we have here evidence of a cult which isn't replicated elsewhere in the south-west. The cave drawings we've found have been interpreted to suggest shamanistic ritual, where it's believed the patient is ill because his soul has been kidnapped . . . taken away by spirits. This has produced unconsciousness or some similar serious disturbance and the shaman's own soul is then induced to enter a trance in order to take flight and retrieve it. Now that's not simple medicine man stuff, where the healer massages, or draws out the illness from a patient by sucking through a straw tube, or produces physical pain in the patient by introducing a foreign object into the patient's body. This is sorcery, black magic . . . this is shamanism.'

'I'm still not clear,' Arnold said. 'You suggest the south-west did not have their shamans?'

Schwartz shrugged. 'What do you mean by a shaman? In ancient cultures they were at once doctors, priests, mystics – even social workers. They seem to be all things to all people and in modern times what precisely they were has occasioned a huge academic debate. But if we look at the origins . . . the word itself comes from the language of the Evenk, hunters and reindeer herders in Siberia, and it was first used to designate a religious specialist from that region. Now it's more widely applied, as we know.'

'Even by New Age travellers in England,' Arnold admitted, thinking of the hairy, unwashed crowds that beseiged Stonehenge at the summer solstice.

Don Schwartz shrugged. 'Is that so . . .? Well, anyway, the soul of the Siberian shaman was said to be able to leave the body and travel to other parts of the cosmos. We would nowadays use the broad definition of a shamanistic culture to include any person who is in *control* of his or her state of trance. Usually involving a soul journey.'

'And such a culture has not been previously discovered in the south-west,' Arnold mused thoughtfully.

'No. Plenty of medicine men and medicine women, yes. But soul flight, no. And in fact there's been a reluctance to admit to that kind of cultural tradition. The last traditional Washo shaman who lived on the California–Nevada border avoided any suggestion of such sorcery – he was better defined as a medicine man. So there we have the puzzle. Here, in the Mojave desert, we have clear evidence of a shamanistic cult involving spirit and soul flight into the cosmos. But how did such a cult get here? Is there any evidence we've missed elsewhere? This is a big task we have here, Mr Landon. There's a deal of work to be done.'

There was something odd in his tone; it was almost as though it contained some kind of challenge.

'You may never find the answer,' Arnold suggested, 'if no other sites are found. Indeed, it might be an isolated, short-lived cult of the kind we see emerging so often in our own modern societies.'

'Don't tell me. We've had enough of that around here.' Schwartz shook his head. 'And yet I have a feeling about this place, Landon. Maybe it's the fact of working here for four years, maybe it's the desert itself, you know? The silence, the distance, the light . . . it can all get to you. I'm convinced there's more to be discovered, answers to be found . . . Anyway, let me show you the rest of the site.'

They moved among the cave dwellings and Schwartz pointed out the various levels of human habitation that had been discovered, talked about the animal bones and artefacts that had been found, and gave them a general history of the Indian people who had lived on this site for generations before they had been uprooted, well before the Spanish conquest, for reasons archaeologists could now only guess at.

'Climatic change?' Arnold ventured.

Schwartz nodded. 'It's one explanation. The collapse of their economy as the land dried out. Maybe agricultural overworking of the soil that led to erosion. Maybe it was an epidemic of some kind or political turmoil – but we've not found too much evidence of warlike characteristics. Anyway, it's too early to come up with a clear hypothesis. Though we have had cranks who've suggested divine wrath, visits by aliens and similar rubbish. Much of it leaning on interpretations of the rock carvings in the shaman's tomb. Irresponsible idiots.'

'It's hardly the way to describe your academic colleagues,' Jane suggested, laughing.

Don Schwartz grinned. 'I wasn't really talking about some of the wilder academic theorists we find on the university circuit. No, it's the others who have got up my nose over the years. There was one group in particular who really annoyed me – they started camping out in the hills near here, and began to interfere with our work with their damned cavortings. Howlings in the night, dancing, incantations, copulations under the desert moon. Depends what turns you on, I suppose, but once we outlined our original findings at this site it was inevitable we got a few nuts jumping out of the log pile.'

'We don't suffer from quite the same thing in England. There are druidic societies and that sort of thing, but they're relatively harmless.'

'That's okay if they don't start diverting attention from the serious work that's going on. But there was one guy who really caused us trouble a couple of years back. I don't know where he drifted from, somewhere east of here I guess, but once he got wind of our findings he tried to set up a cult not far from here. It was all rubbish, of course, and money-orientated: there are always gullible people who're prepared to hand over cash for a supposed trip to the cosmos.'

'He related his cult to the shaman tomb?' Jane asked.

Schwartz nodded. 'It gave him a central point, a focal centre to draw together his following. But it was all a mish-mash. When I said earlier that there's no other evidence of a shamanistic cult in this area I should have intimated also that artefacts were few on the site. Now that isn't the case elsewhere: there's plenty of evidence in the northern sites that the costumes and equipment of a shaman were used to underscore expressive work that began by dance and gesture. Dressing up as an animal, grotesque masks, musical instruments, the shaman's equipment was an extension of his capacity to act. They kept small stones, because rocks were seen as a concentration of power, they used crystals which they regarded as the tears or the semen of sky spirits; they used plants or parts of animals because they could endow the shaman with some of their own properties. But at this site, we have little or no evidence of such equipment.'

'And I suppose some such equipment was inherited,' Arnold suggested.

'That's right,' Schwartz nodded. 'And maybe that was what this damned recent cult that sprang up around here emphasised. Their leader . . . their shaman . . . was claimed to be the inheritor of the ancient cult. But as I said, it was all nonsense, a complete mish-mash. It had nothing that could be described as original or local to this area. If anything the cult was closer to the South American versions – a link with the jaguar, and the use of hallucinogenic drugs.'

'Why the jaguar?' Jane asked.

'It's common in Central and South America. The link arises because the jaguar is a powerful aggressive creature, one which can move freely on land, above ground, and in water, and because it can climb trees in the manner of a shaman's soul.' Schwartz laughed shortly. 'Anyway, it was getting to be a nuisance, because when they set up with their rattles and their incantations and their moonlit seances people started coming along to the site, wanting to peer at the carvings, started suggesting they should be allowed to worship in the chamber. It was at that stage I'd had enough. I wrote an article about the guy eventually, blowing him out of the water, and got into quite a battle with his right-hand man and apologist – a guy called Charlie Jordan. Nasty character.'

'It all died down in due course?'

'Not exactly through my efforts,' Schwartz admitted. 'It was really the IRS who did for him in the end. He scuttled out of here pretty fast, with Jordan on his heels, when some questions were asked about his taxes. I don't know what happened to them –

but no doubt they're practising their trickery elsewhere. There are always gullible people around . . .'

On their last evening at the site they sat on the ridge at sunset in a companionable silence. The colours of the desert were magnificent: tawny reds, gleams of gold, a long rose-pink horizon that changed to a deep blush and fire in the sky. As darkness enclosed the cliff dwellings there was the occasional bark of a coyote in the distance; Schwartz followed his usual practice and lit a pipe. The moon rose and the valley was in deep silvered shadow. They said little, watching the changing scene before them as the moonlight picked out hollows of darkness and the ridges and rocks subtly changed shape before their eyes.

'It's beautiful,' Jane sighed. 'I'm sorry it's time to leave.'

'Mmm.' Don Schwartz glanced quizzically at Arnold. 'Bit different from what you're used to. So tell me a bit more about this work you're involved in up there in the north of England.'

'The Department of Museums and Antiquities is responsible for heritage sites in the county,' Arnold explained. 'I sort of keep an eye on things – overlook sites, maintain liaison with universities working in the area, that sort of thing.'

'She tells me you're lucky with it.'

'I'm not so sure –'

'Aw, come on, we all know the ball game. An experienced archaeologist can work for years and miss things by a hair's breadth. And then some other guy comes along and stumbles over something that's been staring you in the face. I don't decry it: luck is something all archaeologists need. But at what university did you do your training?'

'I've never been to university.'

'I see.'

Schwartz fell silent for a little while. Arnold thought back to his childhood, the long walks he had taken with his father in the Yorkshire Dales, the depth of knowledge his father had demonstrated to him when he talked about the past, the ancient ruined walls, the crumbling stone and the petrified wood. It was his father who had developed in Arnold a love of ancient things, an appreciation, a feel for what had gone before, the mysteries of the past hinted at by ancient remains. He had been lucky after that in the jobs he had gained: the time in the Planning Department had been something of a bore but it had allowed him to develop his skills, his eye for the past, while he continued to extend his own experiences. Now, in the archaeological work he undertook privately, and as part of his job, he felt he had found his niche. Albeit with its own peculiar problems as far as the people he worked with were concerned.

'That's something we're lacking out here right now,' Don Schwartz murmured after a long silence. 'Luck. It's been an interesting site to work on, but this last six months it's as though we've come to a halt. We don't seem to be getting anywhere – there's been nothing of significance to report for a year. There's still a large area to investigate, and I feel sure we'll come up with something, but we still need a wild card, I think, someone with flair . . . Have you ever thought of taking a degree, Landon?'

Surprised, Arnold was silent for a moment. He shrugged. 'I can't say it's really crossed my mind, particularly.'

'You see, if you worked out here with us, under the auspices of the university foundation money, I think we'd have to sort of insist that you took a Master's programme with us. The fact you have no first degree is irrelevant: your experience would allow us to give you direct entry. And it would be by thesis of course, based on work you do at the site. As for financial support, I could probably swing an Associate Professorship for you. Your record speaks for itself: Jane tells me it was you who found the *sudarium* some years back, and there was your work on the Roman and the Celtic sites . . .' Schwartz nodded thoughtfully, musing. 'I don't think it would be a great problem. And we certainly need someone with your kind of luck, and flair . . .'

Arnold was silent, confused by the sudden offer. His mind whirled with the possibilities presented to him. Uncertainly, he said, 'I'm not sure . . . this is something of a surprise. I'm just out here on holiday. I hadn't really even thought about –'

Don Schwartz turned his heavy head to look at Arnold. His pipe glowed as he drew on it, and his eyes seemed to glitter. 'But Jane was telling me . . . I understood you might be interested in working out here.'

23

Arnold was aware of Jane tensing, sitting beside him. She said nothing. Arnold was silent for a little while. 'To be honest, I'd not really contemplated such an idea. I'm fascinated by the site, and realise the challenge out here, and I'm very interested by what you have to say, and flattered that you think I might have a contribution to make. But it's all something of a surprise and it would need a great deal of thinking about.'

There was a short silence. 'Of course,' Schwartz replied quietly. He glanced at Jane, seemed about to say something and then thought better of it. He tapped out his pipe on the rock in front of him. The silence now held an edge of tension, and embarrassment, and Schwartz was perhaps aware that he had spoken out of turn. He cleared his throat awkwardly, and grunted. 'Well, folks, it's an early start in the morning if we're to get you to the airport in time. I guess I'll turn in. Dream well.'

He rose to his feet clumsily, and made his way back to his tent. There was a coolness in the air and Arnold sat silently for a little while staring out over the moonlit desert. Jane sat stiffly beside him, her face averted. At last Arnold asked, 'So what exactly was that all about?'

'I've been meaning to bring it up with you,' she said awkwardly. 'Don sort of . . . jumped the gun.'

'On the last evening here? You've had plenty of time to warn me.'

'It wasn't like that! I wanted him to meet you, and I told him about you, the work you'd done, and he seemed interested so I sort of broached the subject with him –'

'Without consulting me.'

'Well, yes, but I thought . . . well, I knew you'd find the site interesting, and the challenge one that would stretch your imagination, and I've heard about some of the problems you've had over the years in Northumberland. I just thought this would be a great opportunity . . .'

'Which it is,' Arnold said slowly. 'But it's been rather sprung on me. And the university thing . . .' He shook his head doubtfully. 'It's all so sudden, a surprise, and I don't know . . .'

'Don Schwartz likes you. He thinks he could work with you.

24

This could be fantastic, an opportunity, Arnold, to do something entirely different –'

'I don't dispute that. But if you knew it was in the wind, why didn't you mention it to me before?'

She was silent for a little while. Then she sighed. 'Look, I'd better come clean. It's been on my mind for a while. Coming out here, to the States, in the first instance it was an excitement for me. Film deals, television options, there's a hunger out here for my work that I don't experience back in England. The way things are going out here I'm busy, exhilarated, challenged. And you're back in Northumberland.'

She turned her head to look at him. 'We haven't seen each other in a while, Arnold. I wondered whether things were the same between us, or whether there's been a change, as a result of our being apart. But I don't think anything *has* changed, has it?'

'I don't know what you mean,' he replied quietly.

'I think you do. I still detect no sort of . . . commitment.' She took a deep breath. 'So, I thought maybe this was one way to find out how the land lay. I suggested you came out to join me for a couple of weeks. I introduced you to Don Schwartz. I told him all about you, brought you out to this site, and he's impressed enough to make the suggestions he did.'

'Influenced by you?'

'I talked to him, yes,' she replied defiantly. 'The point is, it would work, Arnold. It would give you a new, exciting challenge, and a new environment. And I'd know where I stand.'

'What exactly do you mean by that, Jane?'

'I'd know what you wanted. I'd know that you wanted to be near me. I can't see myself coming back to England, not the way things are going. My future's here in the States. Yours could be too. If you wanted it enough. If you wanted to be with *me* enough.'

There was no mistaking the ultimatum in her tone. Arnold stared out over the silvered landscape. 'This is something I'd need time to consider.'

'That's an answer in itself.'

'No. Not exactly. But there are things to consider . . . this would be an uprooting –'

'Don't wait too long to decide, Arnold,' she said crisply, scrambling to her feet. 'I can't imagine Don will be too happy with any great delay. It's a generous offer he's made.'

He rose with her, awkwardly. 'Jane –'

'And I'd like to know fairly soon, too.'

2

Inevitably, there was a stack of work waiting for Arnold when he returned to his office in Morpeth. His desk was covered in files and memos so during the greater part of the first morning back at work he was busy sorting it all into some kind of order of priority. Naturally, there were several sharp-toned notes from Karen Stannard – she had the capacity to identify problems that seemed to arise only as a result of his absence, every time he was absent. And she seemed to take a considerable pleasure in informing him of it.

Particularly so now that she was acting head of the Department of Museums and Antiquities. The last few months had been a difficult time for everyone in the department. The death of the former director, Simon Brent-Ellis, had caused turmoil which was not alleviated by the failure of the council to appoint his deputy, Karen Stannard, to the post. She felt she deserved it but the promotion had been withheld – and she retained the unreasonable suspicion that Arnold had had something to do with it. She was also still firmly convinced that he wanted the job for himself, which was far from the truth. But it had all conspired to make the temporary regime a somewhat uncomfortable one to work under.

Arnold was a little surprised that the call did not come until shortly before lunchtime. The phone buzzed, he picked up the receiver, and a crisp tone informed him that he was required to call at the office of Miss Karen Stannard. Gloomily, Arnold shuffled through the various memoranda on his desk, picked out those he had decided were priority and slipped them into a manila file cover. He closed his office door behind him.

The director's office was at the end of the corridor. There had previously been an ante-room to the left where the redoubtable Cerberus, Miss Sansom, had been wont to snarl at visitors before allowing them to enter the presence of her beloved director. After Brent-Ellis's death she had been dispensed with and now worked in the Chief Executive's department. The office itself had been refurbished and Arnold now saw that there was a name plate on the door: *Assistant to the Director*. He grimaced. He had known the appointment was due to be made when he was leaving for the States. It looked as though it had all happened.

Arnold tapped on the door of the director's office. There was a brief silence, and then he heard Karen Stannard's voice, inviting him to enter. He sighed: it hadn't been that way in Miss Sansom's day. Somehow, he missed the snarling antagonism.

Karen Stannard had rearranged Simon Brent-Ellis's room. The former director had liked to have his desk alongside the window so he could stare out at the distant golf course he loved so well. Miss Stannard was more businesslike – she had moved the desk so that her back was to the light, a new bookshelf had appeared in the room, the chairs had been renewed and the office redecorated to a more subtle, feminine shade. She had been busy during Arnold's absence.

She noted his glancing around the room and she smiled. 'You like it?'

'It's different. I'm amazed you got Direct Works to move so fast.'

The smile was lazy, almost feline in its satisfaction. 'I made the point to the people who matter that it was important to change the . . . atmosphere of the room, after Mr Brent-Ellis's unfortunate demise. And, of course, a little femininity would not come amiss . . .'

It was part of her weaponry, of course. Arnold looked at her: he had almost forgotten how impossibly beautiful she was. She sat leaning back in her chair now, the top button of her white blouse open to display a tanned throat, the long, slim fingers of her right hand toying with a pencil on the desk in front of her. Her skin was perfect, her mouth confident and her eyes were shaded, their green – or was it hazel? – half hidden by drooping, casual lids. The room would be part of a planned background, a

27

set in which she would be able to make best advantage of her appearance and her skills. She was manipulative, controlled, and at her most dangerous when she appeared at ease.

'So, Mr Landon, you've deigned to return to us at last.'

'It was only two weeks. I had it due to me.'

'If you hadn't,' she purred, 'I wouldn't have allowed you to go, as a senior member of this department. But let's be clear, it was my decision as director – because it was not the most convenient of times to be short-handed in the department.' She stretched her long body languidly. 'Things have been pretty hectic during your absence.'

'So I can guess.' He waved the manila folder. 'I've had a quick look at the memos you've sent me –'

'I'm sure you'll deal with them as quickly as you're able. But that's not why I called you in.. I thought it would be useful if you were to make the early acquaintance of my new assistant.' She smiled at Arnold, and pressed the buzzer on her desk. 'Portia, would you like to come in for a few minutes?'

She raised an eyebrow and the smile became even more feline and self-satisfied. 'Portia Tyrrel. I'm sure you'll enjoy working with her.'

A few moments later the door opened and the new assistant to the director walked in. Arnold turned, and stared. Whatever he had been expecting it was certainly not the sight of the woman who had entered the room.

Arnold had a view of Karen Stannard. She was a beautiful, calculating, very professional woman whose ambition drove her hard, sometimes into making misjudgements about people – not least about Arnold himself. She knew how to handle men so that she got what she wanted from them, and she was sufficiently egotistical to enjoy the attention her appearance aroused – and use that attention to the best purpose for the advancement of her own career. There were rumours that she had lesbian tendencies, but Arnold put that down to the fact of unsuccessful raids on her virtue by the Lotharios of the department. But he was surprised now to feel that he had misjudged her in one matter at least: he had never believed that she would have allowed another strikingly beautiful woman to work closely with her in the department.

28

And Portia Tyrrel was beautiful. Not in the same way as Karen Stannard, whose tall, confident, almost arrogant beauty caused heads to swivel in every conference room she entered. But eyes would follow Portia Tyrrel also. For she was small and slim, perhaps only five feet two in height; her hair was short and black, fringed at the front, and her skin was a pale olive, her eyes luminous and slanting. She wore a high-necked shirt, a dark, formal skirt to the knee; she was small-breasted, slimly built, and she moved with an easy confidence. She was Euro-Asian, Arnold guessed, and beautiful to Western eyes, as those women who seemed to possess the advantages of both races always were.

She held out a slim hand, and smiled: she had perfect teeth. 'Mr Landon. I've heard a great deal about you. I look forward to our working together.'

Her accent offered no clue as to her origins. Arnold opened his mouth to say something, but there seemed nothing appropriate to say. As he stammered, Karen Stannard enjoyed the moment.

'Why don't you sit down, both of you?' she suggested. 'There are some things we need to talk about. And Mr Landon needs time to get his breath back now he's become aware he will be completely hag-ridden from now on.'

Hag-ridden . . . hardly. But Arnold dragged his eyes away from Portia Tyrrel and pulled a chair forward for her, then took one himself. There was a short silence as Karen Stannard eyed him with a malicious mischievousness, and her assistant sat demurely with lowered eyes, waiting.

'We've been fortunate with the appointment of Miss Tyrrel,' Karen Stannard announced at last. 'As you know, Landon, there's been a certain down-sizing here at the department since Mr Brent-Ellis . . . passed on. I let the Chief Executive know that with certain reorganisation I could manage to run the department quite effectively with fewer staff. He was happy to concur with that decision, of course . . .'

Naturally. It saved money, and it was his idea anyway. Karen Stannard could not have argued about it, if she wanted to retain any hope of being created permanent head of the department.

'But my . . . elevation to this office meant that while I felt there was no need to replace myself, so to speak, with a deputy, I would nevertheless need the services of an assistant. A post

29

I could not ask *you* to undertake, of course, in view of your already heavy commitments.'

Her eyes were definitely green, and smoky in their expression. Arnold shifted uneasily in his seat, and glanced at the woman seated beside him. Her features were composed, her eyes still lowered. 'I'm pleased Miss Tyrrel was able to take up the post so quickly.'

'That's where we've been so fortunate,' Karen Stannard said airily. 'Portia was immediately available because she had just finished a stint of post-graduate work at Cambridge. She comes to us with glowing credentials: her doctorate material is to be published during the course of the year by a leading international house and she has already established a reputation for herself in . . . what was it exactly?'

Portia Tyrrel allowed herself a tiny smile. 'The symbolism of votive objects in Celtic and Romano-British cultures.'

'Ah, yes, you must forgive me . . . It's certainly an area in which we lack expertise, and I'm sure that Arnold will learn a great deal from you as you work together.' The flash of her smile towards Arnold removed none of the bite from the words. 'I have it in mind, you see, that you two should work closely together. I quickly discovered, after I took over the department a few months ago, that the external demands on my time are rapidly increasing, not least because of our successful bids for Lottery money. Consequently, my idea of the kind of person I felt I needed as my assistant changed quite significantly, especially when Portia applied for the job. She made quite an impression at interview . . . not least among the councillors . . .'

Arnold wasn't surprised.

'And when they discovered her qualifications – Oxford degree, Cambridge research, experience on the Frenchay project in Hertfordshire –' Karen Stannard waved an elegant, negligent hand, 'they very quickly agreed that the job description should be changed. And I was personally delighted when it became clear that she could join us immediately. Appointed just ten days ago . . . and here she is!'

Arnold inclined his head in Portia Tyrrel's direction. 'I hope you'll be very happy here.'

'I'm sure I shall be,' she breathed with muted enthusiasm.

There was an expression of controlled satisfaction on Karen Stannard's features. The wicked glint in her eyes was not lost to Arnold. 'So,' she went on, 'the change in job description, which I wasn't able to discuss with you, Arnold, since you were on leave in the States, means that Portia will be taking on rather more . . . ah . . . responsibility from me than had originally been intended. Rather than merely act as my assistant in the day-to-day running of the department, it was decided, after consultation with the Chief Executive, that she should be given a more, shall we say, *substantive* role?'

Arnold could guess what was coming.

'It's been decided that Portia should report direct to me on the operation of the antiquities side of our work. It's the area in which you've been most involved of course, Arnold, and this in no way means that Miss Tyrrel is being brought in above your head. Of course not, you still remain a senior and valued member of the department and will continue to undertake the work you've been doing. But you never did care much for the office side of things, did you? This arrangement will mean you'll have more time for field work . . . which is what you enjoy doing, isn't it?' The claws were unsheathed just a little for a moment. 'And it does mean you and I don't need to see as much of each other also, as has been the case in the past.'

Slowly, Arnold said, 'I think it would be useful if Miss Tyrrel's duties could be spelled out a little more clearly –'

'Oh, I'll be sending out a memo, Arnold, don't worry about it,' Karen Stannard interrupted airily. 'But in general, it will mean that your reports in future can go to Portia rather than direct to me, and I'll be rearranging some of your committee work – she can take over some of the more irksome activities that have dragged you from the field research. And that'll suit everyone, won't it?'

There was a short silence. At last, Arnold said, 'Well, if that's all, I've got quite a bit of work to do, catching up on what's landed on my desk in my absence.'

A vague shadow of disappointment touched Karen Stannard's mouth. Arnold had not reacted in the manner she had clearly hoped he would. 'Yes, all right, in a moment. But there's one other thing I need to mention before you return to your office. You know Colonel McArdle?'

Arnold shook his head. 'I don't think so . . .'

'He's been pestering us for some time. He's chairman of an antiquarian society based up at Amble of all places, and he's been wanting someone from the department to give a talk on the work we do in support of local societies with reference to some of our own activities in the field. He's been after me for a while, but I really don't have time – now that I'm running this department – so I think it would be a good idea if you were to get in touch with him, Arnold, and take on the job. Portia should go along with you. It will give her the chance to see a little of the countryside, get her bearings and all that, and she'll learn a little more about the department as well.'

'If you give me the details,' Arnold said a little stiffly, 'I'll see what can be arranged.'

'Yes . . . Portia will bring them to you.' Karen Stannard eyed Arnold thoughtfully for a few seconds and then, as he slowly rose to his feet, she glanced at her assistant. 'I think that'll be all for now, Portia. Perhaps you could leave us now – there's a couple more things I need to discuss with Mr Landon . . .'

Portia Tyrrel rose smoothly, gave Arnold a demure smile, and left the room. Arnold watched her go, and then, still on his feet, turned back to face the acting head of the department. She was staring at him quizzically. After a short silence, she said, 'I've got the full support of the committee and the council in all this, you know.'

'I'm sure you have.'

'You haven't reacted the way I thought you would. You're non-committal. I'd like a view, Arnold.'

'A view? About what?' Arnold smiled thinly. 'You and the appointments committee have reached a decision. And as you rightly say, by bringing in Miss Tyrrel and giving her senior responsibilities it will leave me more time to do the field work that I'm happy doing.'

'So you've no complaints.'

'I'm making none.'

'That's a little . . . evasive. And I've always seen you as a straight-talking man.'

'I don't know whether that's true. You certainly have held some rather strange views about me.'

'I've never *trusted* you, that's for sure.' She shook her head, a little puzzled. 'I never quite know what you're up to, what makes you tick. Sometimes I think you play things straight, but on other occasions . . . One thing I'm certain of. You want this job.'

'You're wrong.'

'You don't fool me, Arnold. You're good, your experience is excellent, you've overcome all the disadvantages of having no academic background, but you're ambitious, too. Oh, you hide it very well, but I've known men like you before. You're good at dissembling, at pulling the wool over people's eyes. But not mine, never mine!'

'Is there anything else?' Arnold asked curtly.

Karen Stannard appeared frustrated at his lack of response. She leaned forward, her eyes dark now, shadowed with anger. 'All right, let's have it out in the open. I know you were disappointed when I was given this job – albeit in an acting capacity! No, don't bother trying to deny it. I got it, and I intend making it my own! But you would always be a threat and I know it: you have supporters among the other officers, not least with that stuffed shirt of a Chief Executive Powell Frinton – ah, don't affect to be surprised!'

Arnold was. He had always felt Powell Frinton disapproved of him.

'So let's be absolutely clear. When I saw what Portia Tyrrel could offer us, I jumped at the opportunity presented. I'm uneasy with you around me, Landon; I know you're breathing down my neck. And I'm not handing this department to you on a plate. Your protestations are false; I don't believe them. But this way I can emasculate you. Once she knows this department, she'll make you dispensable. And that will suit me fine.'

'I'm not going to argue with you, Miss Stannard. You're right – I'll be happier working away from the office. But you're wrong about my perceived ambitions. Still, it's no matter.' He turned, and began to walk towards the door. Then, unaccountably, he stopped and looked back at her. Coldly, he added, 'I might well be leaving anyway.'

For a moment she seemed hardly to understand what he had said. Then she stared at him and her mouth opened slightly, her eyes widened. 'What do you mean?'

'While I was on holiday in the States I had a job offer.'

'You're not serious. What kind of a job?'

'The University of New Mexico. Working on a dig in the Mojave desert. And improving somewhat on the academic qualifications you quite rightly point out I'm lacking in.'

'New Mexico? You're being *headhunted* for a job in New Mexico?' She glared at him in frustration as she struggled with the mixture of emotions that affected her. 'But you can't –'

'Nothing's fixed yet, of course,' Arnold said coolly. 'But if and when it happens, you'll be the first to know.'

He had never seen her look so deflated in all the time he had known her at the department.

Back in the quiet of his own room he felt deflated himself. Karen Stannard had caught him on the raw: her appointment of Portia Tyrrel had been a surprise, and in many ways she had been right in her cynical explanation that it would suit him, give him more time for field work, permit him to avoid the office work he found irritating. But he was annoyed and confused because of the fury he felt at recognising the motives that lay behind the appointment. Karen Stannard saw him as a threat, and this was her way of negating that threat, interposing a layer of responsibility between herself and him, downgrading him in the eyes of the councillors, appointing someone, moreover, who would quickly obtain their male support, always open as they were to manipulation by an attractive woman.

But he was also disgusted with himself for feeling these emotions. He was not ambitious. His job suited him. He had no desire to take Karen Stannard's job. And yet he hated being outmanoeuvred in this way.

Not that there was much he was able to do about it; nothing he was *prepared* to do about it. She was welcome to the director's job. Yet suddenly, the prospect of working in the Mojave desert had become considerably more attractive.

There was a light tap on the door. It opened and Portia Tyrrel stood framed in the doorway, calm and level-eyed. She held a folder in her left hand. She came forward and placed it on the desk in front of him. 'It's the information about Colonel McArdle's antiquarian society. But the society's based at Wark, not Amble. I thought you might need it. And you'll let me know what arrangements you'll be making, if I'm to come with you.'

He nodded. She smiled faintly and turned to leave. As she was closing the door behind her she looked back. Her features were suddenly very Chinese, he thought. 'That meeting,' she said quietly. 'Lot of bullshit, wasn't it?'

In spite of his suppressed anger, Arnold smiled.

3

The seminar room was small, narrow and recently decorated: the hot sun that slanted in through the high window overlooking the lawns and walkways of the university campus glowed on the pale green-painted walls and seemed to accentuate the smell of the paint, sickly in Inspector O'Connor's nostrils. He glanced around him: the room was clearly used for small groups of students since there was only the one long table and six chairs. He wondered at the kind of university economics that would allow for such small teaching groups and he walked across to the window. Small teaching groups, green lawns, an artificial stream and lake, trees . . . life was easy for these students. Disgruntled suddenly, he wondered how it was his own life had taken the turns it had. He could have gone to university. Instead, he'd followed in his father's footsteps. A copper.

His faint reflection in the window gazed back at him unblinkingly. Lean, tall, saturnine of features, dark-haired and discontented. Very much like his father had been, he thought . . . but at least Jack O'Connor Junior had made inspector while the old man had never made it beyond sergeant.

He turned away as the door opened behind him.

Dr James Satterthwaite was small, plump, fussy in his mannerisms and inclined to be rather self-important in his speech. But he seemed to like Jack O'Connor and when liaison work of this kind was called for, he always seemed pleased to help as far as he could, although his reputation with other liaison officers was not good. He could be sharp-tongued, cutting in his comments, and there were rumours about his possible sexual preferences. But he always seemed prepared to put himself out for O'Connor. Maybe he liked the Irish ... even though Jack O'Connor was really a Lancashire lad, his Irish origins buried in three generations of life in the north of England. But O'Connor could put on a passable brogue when required. He did so now.

'It's pleased I am to see you, Doc.'

Satterthwaite beamed and scuttled forward to shake O'Connor's hand, pumping it enthusiastically, before settling himself into a chair and depositing a pile of papers on the table in front of him. 'I'm sorry to drag you out here like this, Jack, but my university commitments are such that I'm not going to be able to get back to the forensic labs for the rest of the week and I know you like to have my personal views about work you put on my slabs.' He chuckled and winked. 'And of course, you always want the information yesterday ... but I understand that.'

'I don't mind the trip,' O'Connor replied. 'Gets me away from my usual haunts.'

'How's your father, Jack?'

'He's managing,' O'Connor replied carefully. He could have spoken of senility, of Alzheimer's, of the dreariness of a nursing home and the reflections of a ravaged memory in a crumbling face.

'Well, give him my regards ... You know, he brought me one of the first jobs I ever had to do as a forensic scientist.'

'A long while ago ...' O'Connor paused. 'And what about this latest job?'

Satterthwaite leaned back in his chair, folded his pudgy hands across his paunch and frowned reflectively. 'Well, Jack, I have to tell you it's going to be a difficult one. There are certain things we can be fairly sure of. First, the fact he was male.' He chuckled sardonically. 'The fish didn't do much damage in the testicular direction. The fact he was maybe thirty, thirty-five years of age. Well-built but his muscular development would not suggest manual labour. He'd eaten fish before he died, which means they got their own back on him in the end, doesn't it?' He gave a macabre chuckle.

O'Connor wrinkled his nose – he'd always been of the opinion that forensic scientists had a peculiar sense of humour. Maybe it was a defence mechanism on their part.

'But setting that aside,' Satterthwaite continued, 'we don't have a great deal to go on. Immersion in the sea for a period of time –'

'How long?'

'Ten days, couple of weeks, I would guess. Such an immersion unfortunately removed most of the information we might have been able to rely on.'

'Cause of death?'

'Difficult.' Satterthwaite pursed rosy, thoughtful lips and scratched his nose. 'He didn't drown ... that we can establish. No particular signs of violence on his body apart from the one I'll describe in a moment. So no obvious clues as to whether it was a suicide or a homicide. The problem is, the head and hands, you see.'

'Identification is possible from the wallet we found on the body, but cause of death ...'

'Well, Jack, you've been in the business long enough to know that teeth can help and fingerprints can help but not if both have been removed. There is a question in my mind of course ... was the head removed before the body hit the water?'

'And?'

'Difficult to say. The fishing vessel ... Spanish, wasn't it? The screws somewhat mangled the neck area and probably took off the head, though it's possible the fish had already done that anyway. As for the hands ... the lacerations on the bone of the left wrist and on the neck and shoulder area are consistent with both head and hand having been removed by the contact with the ship propellers, and the fingertips of the other hand were certainly eaten away by marine animals.' Satterthwaite sucked at his lips. 'There's not much more I can tell you.'

37

'But if he wasn't drowned he could have been dead before he went into the water so it could have been murder?'

'Can't really give you an opinion, to be frank. Someone could have strangled him, say, or killed him with a blow to the head . . . but with the head gone, I couldn't in all conscience give you an opinion. And he could have been alive in the water and been struck accidentally by some other vessel . . . can't really tell, can we? And as to confirming his identity, no fingerprints, no teeth . . . I guess on this occasion forensically I'm not going to be able to help you very much at all.'

So O'Connor's journey to the university had been of little assistance. Something of the thought must have been apparent from his face, because Satterthwaite leaned forward anxiously. 'But of course, I thought you'd want to know one way or the other, without having to wait for the official report from the labs. They do tend to take rather a long time.'

Satterthwaite laid a sympathetic hand on O'Connor's wrist. It lay there, warm and pudgy, for perhaps a couple of seconds longer than it should have. O'Connor shifted uncomfortably. There was a warmth in his chest, subdued anger and annoyance.

He'd always seen himself as a man's man, but suddenly the phrase seemed to possess a certain ambiguity.

The thought that he had wasted his time stayed with him when he drove back to York. The traffic was heavy, as it usually was, so it was late afternoon before he arrived at the office. There was a message waiting for him at the desk, when he entered the reception area.

'Chief superintendent?' O'Connor raised his eyebrows. 'What's he want?'

He didn't wait for an answer but headed for the stairs.

Chief Superintendent Jenkins was seated in his office with a visitor and two cups of tea. His bald head glistened as he looked up at O'Connor and gestured to him to take a seat. He made no attempt to offer O'Connor any refreshment, but then, the two men did not get on. There had been bad blood between Jenkins and Jack O'Connor Senior in the old days when they had been on the beat together. O'Connor guessed that his father had put the rookie Jenkins through some kind of alley baptism in the back streets of Middlesbrough, but the old man had never talked about it. Whatever the cause, a streak of resentment had remained in Jenkins and had found fresh life when the younger O'Connor had joined the force.

'Anything useful to report?' he asked brusquely, a slight emphasis on the word 'useful' suggesting he placed little reliance on O'Connor's judgement or capability.

O'Connor shook his head. 'Wasted journey, really. Dr Satterthwaite reckons there'll be little we'll glean from the corpse.'

'Then maybe it's just as well that we have Inspector Garcia here to help us out, isn't it?' Jenkins suggested sardonically.

The other man in the room rose to his feet, putting down his cup on Jenkins's desk. He turned to face O'Connor, holding out his hand in greeting. 'You'll be Inspector O'Connor,' he said in perfectly accented English. 'The chief superintendent has been telling me that you're in charge of the investigation into the death of the man found in the sea off Robin Hood's Bay.'

'That's right,' O'Connor replied, noting the firmness of Garcia's handshake.

'Inspector Garcia is some way out of his jurisdiction,' Jenkins said heavily, 'but thinks he might be able to help us.' His tone implied his doubts on the matter, but then, Jenkins had always been somewhat parochial in his attitudes.

O'Connor appraised the man standing in front of him. Garcia was of middle height, immaculately dressed in a well-cut dark suit and grey and black tie. His skin was tanned, his eyes the kind of deep, intelligent brown that women would swoon over. His dark hair was frosted at the temples with grey. He had an easy manner, and a swift smile, but there was a hint of arrogance in his jaw, and O'Connor guessed he would not be a man to be trifled with. As he sat down again O'Connor himself took a chair.

'You're with the Spanish police?' O'Connor asked.

Garcia smiled. 'Not exactly. I work for Interpol. And at the moment I'm doing a certain liaison job, trying to fit together a picture about the man who was fished out of the sea. The jurisdiction over the death would seem to be yours, of course . . . but when as a matter of routine the man's name was sent to Interpol, it was suggested that I should come and see you.'

Jenkins grunted unpleasantly. 'As you know, O'Connor, Interpol is really an information agency. Not real, active coppers.'

The chief superintendent had made no attempt to hide the sneer, but Garcia ignored it and took no offence openly. He held O'Connor's glance. 'I gather you've been talking to the forensic scientists at York today. Have you any further information?'

O'Connor shrugged. 'Not really. Nothing to confirm or otherwise the identity of the man.'

'Which was obtained from information in his wallet and body belt,' Garcia glanced keenly at O'Connor. 'What about the cause of death?'

'Can't be specific. Could have been suicide; could have been accidental; nothing positive to suggest murder. Except that the man did not drown. Which would suggest that he may well have come to a sticky end before he entered the water.' O'Connor hesitated, watching Garcia carefully. 'But if Interpol have something on the man, it would suggest he's been involved in criminal activity of some kind.'

There was a short pause, then Garcia nodded. 'That's right: you might say that with confidence. When the body was fished out of the sea you found some documentation – in the body belt. The details have been passed to Interpol – they suggest that the dead man was Timothy James Brazil. The name is certainly known to Interpol. Indeed, we have been working closely with the Spanish police out of Barcelona for some time in connection with Timothy Brazil.'

'What's he been up to?'

Garcia gave an expressive shrug of his shoulders. 'Many things. Mr Brazil has been active on the fringe of the criminal underworld for many years, it would seem. But he's either been very clever, or very lucky.'

'Luck's run out now,' Jenkins grunted.

Garcia flashed the chief superintendent a cool smile and turned back to O'Connor. 'We think that Brazil was involved in various things over the years, such as prostitution, gaming clubs, the usual lines one expects to see with the kind of man who is looking for – as the Americans say – a quick buck. But a few years ago he became more ambitious, developed his connections in South-East Asia and Africa and . . . You will be aware, I've no doubt, that there is a drug-running line in from Morocco to the northern coast of Spain. The distance is very short . . . a dark night, a fast boat, a long coastline difficult to police . . .'

Chief Superintendent Jenkins caught O'Connor's eye and raised an eyebrow, suggesting he had a certain view of the efficiency of the Spanish police.

'Brazil was involved in drug running?' O'Connor asked.

'Most certainly. A significant dossier had been built up on him. He was not exactly a major player, but he was big enough for us to have an interest in him. But then, while we have been keeping surveillance on him, making sure we could get him *in flagrante* so to speak, we detected a certain nervousness in him and his operations. As far as we can gather, there was some kind of trouble within the syndicate he was involved with. Informants would suggest that Brazil had become too greedy . . . maybe he had upset his colleagues. What is clear is that he dropped out of sight for a while, after receiving a visit from some Americans . . . presumably people also involved in the syndicate, though we have little information on them.'

'You think this . . . trouble . . . might have led to Brazil's murder?' O'Connor asked.

'Of that we cannot be sure.' Garcia smiled thinly. 'Let's just say that we became very interested when we heard that his body had been fished out of the sea. We had thought earlier that maybe he had found some way of . . . disappearing from the consequences of his actions. Death was . . . drastic.'

'How do you mean?'

Garcia scratched thoughtfully at his cheek with a lean finger. 'Timothy Brazil was American by birth, but he had lived in Holland and Germany for some years before setting up head-quarters in Barcelona. He first came to our attention about three years ago, but his operation was soundly run and it was difficult to pin anything on him. We were getting close, through inform-ants, intelligence picked up in Marseilles and Algiers. However, during the three years of his involvement in the drug trade he certainly was making a great deal of money out of his activities

41

and he had enough money to collect the trappings of success. One such instance of ostentatious wealth was called the *Dawn Princess*.'

'A yacht?'

Garcia nodded. 'Ocean-going. She was berthed at Santander, on the northern coast of Spain. And two weeks ago she left Santander suddenly, at night. And vanished.'

'Slipped up there, didn't you,' Jenkins sneered, 'if you were supposed to be keeping tag on him.'

'There were certain . . . errors,' Garcia agreed mildly. 'But the fact is he probably knew the nets were closing in on him and he decided to vanish – from us, and maybe from his colleagues as well.'

'He didn't seem to have got far,' O'Connor remarked grimly.

'As I say, the *Dawn Princess* vanished. We got no sightings after she was observed leaving harbour. No landings, no coastguard reports, no distress calls.'

'But now, a body.' O'Connor frowned, thinking. 'You think she was sunk?'

Garcia shrugged. 'There is always that possibility. But was it done deliberately? Was it an accident? Was it murder?'

'And if it *was* murder, who killed Mr Brazil?'

'This accounts for our interest,' Garcia smiled. 'And why I'm here. To assist with any information I can give you. Mr Brazil . . . he was one of my case files. So though I'm not an *active* policeman, I may be able to help.'

Jenkins shuffled impatiently in his seat. 'I don't know that we can give this matter a high priority. O'Connor can stick with it for the time being, but it seems to me that if this dead man was as big a rogue as you make out –'

'Was Brazil alone on the boat?' O'Connor interrupted.

Garcia shook his head. 'We believe there were at least three men on board.'

'Three men, one corpse.'

'The others might still be feeding the fishes,' Jenkins muttered.

Garcia nodded, but managed to demonstrate a lack of conviction in the suggestion. 'That may well be so . . . But in our

42

surveillance we noted the arrival of the two Americans, and we think they might both have travelled with Brazil to the *Dawn Princess*. The strange thing is, we have reason to believe that the one American whose identity we *have* ascertained left Spain three days after the *Dawn Princess* sailed. We raided Brazil's apartment and found certain information that suggested his American colleague had booked a flight out of Valencia. Unfortunately, the information came into our possession too late: he had taken the flight. We would have liked to talk to him, because, of course, if he travelled to Santander with Brazil, and if he boarded the *Dawn Princess*, and yet came back to Spain at some point very quickly afterwards, only to leave again by air, it's possible he'd have some information for us about what actually happened to Brazil's yacht in the interim –'

'And what happened to Timothy Brazil.'

'Precisely. And who knows where that might lead?'

There was a short silence. Chief Superintendent Jenkins cleared his throat noisily. 'All right, I think that's as far as we can go right now. O'Connor ... as you know, we've more than enough on already, but you're assigned to this matter until notice is given otherwise. Which could be sooner than later. And Inspector Garcia ...' Jenkins hooded his eyes as he stared at the Interpol officer. '... Inspector Garcia will be around to help. Until his masters call him back to heel.'

Outside Jenkins's office O'Connor glanced at Garcia and shrugged. 'Sorry about that, Inspector –'

'Raoul.'

'Okay,' O'Connor smiled. 'Where do you want to start?'

Surprisingly, Garcia said, 'With a beer. Isn't that how working friendships always begin in England?'

PART TWO

1

Arnold had visited a supervised excavation at a Roman bridge site on the fells above the North Tyne in the early morning so he was rather pushed for time when he arrived at the office to pick up Portia Tyrrel: he explained that he had to attend a meeting with the Clerk to the Council at Alnwick over the lunch period, after which they would proceed to Warkworth where he was due to give the late afternoon talk to Colonel McArdle's antiquarian group, as a stand-in for Karen Stannard. He suggested that there was no point in Portia attending his lunchtime meeting at Alnwick, but she could take advantage of the opportunity to wander around the town for an hour or so before they made their way south-east to Warkworth. She readily agreed and they set off immediately. At Alnwick Arnold dropped her off near the market hall and arranged to meet her again on the Lion Bridge.

His meeting was somewhat protracted, and not particularly useful. He felt a little guilty at the thought of Portia Tyrrel waiting for him so at the conclusion of the meeting he hurried away. She was waiting at the Lion Bridge as agreed. He pulled up and apologised for being late as she got into the passenger seat. 'You managed to get some lunch?' he asked.

'In the hotel – a quick snack.'

'And you've done the tourist bit?'

She laughed; it was a light, friendly sound. 'I've done Bondgate and the Hotspur Gate; I've seen the gatehouse of the Premonstratensian abbey, and I've clambered the ruins of Hulne Priory. I've also viewed the castle from all angles.' The road looped southwards as they drove, and the castle was to their right, just behind them. Portia looked back with a small smile on her lips. 'Magnificent location.'

'The Percys always chose well.'

'And built well, it seems. What is it, twelfth-century?'

Arnold nodded. 'With a history of sieges by the Scots. The

interior was remodelled in the eighteenth century – the keep chambers in Robert Adam designs, and then in the nineteenth century, after a disastrous fire, Italian craftsmen were called in to create a suite of state rooms with classical decoration. And the park you walked in, by the way, to see the priory, was land-scaped by Capability Brown.'

'Are castles your hobby?' she asked curiously.

'I wouldn't say that. But if you're interested in medieval wood and stone, well, you can hardly ignore castles, can you? After all, most of the buildings of the past have long since disappeared – it's only those which were built in an uneconomic way, by people who could afford to spend a lot of money on them, which have survived. And plenty of money was spent on Alnwick – it had the advantage of a considerable strengthening in the four-teenth century by the Percys, so that it became one of the chief border fortresses.'

'And the figures on the parapets?'

'Eighteenth-century, but my guess is they replaced medieval originals.'

They drove on, leaving Alnwick behind them. They left the A1 and struck eastwards towards the coast; at their backs the Cheviots were shrouded in lowering rain clouds but patches of sunshine brightened the road ahead and they caught occasional glimpses of the dark blue of the North Sea where the River Coquet flowed past Amble.

'So have you settled in now?' Arnold asked after a while.

She turned her almond eyes upon him. 'To the department? Yes, more or less.'

'What made you take up a career in archaeology?' he asked curiously.

Portia Tyrrel laughed. 'Bloody-mindedness, I think. My father was from Scotland originally but for most of his working life he was based in Hong Kong and Singapore, working as a corporate lawyer. That's when he met my mother – she was Singaporean. And he was ambitious for me. Sent me to school in England, at Roedean of all places! And then there was Oxford for my first degree, Cambridge for research . . . He had wanted me to follow in his shadow, and go into law as well.'

'So that's the reason for Portia.'

'I imagine so. But, as children often do, I suppose, I kicked against the traces, and turned to history. He was furious. Said there was no money in it.'

'He was right.'

She glanced at him again, a serious expression on her face. 'But money isn't what it's all about, necessarily. I mean, *you're* a happy man in the work you do, aren't you?'

He shrugged. 'I suppose I am. I'm doing what I want; and I'm able to work in one of the most beautiful counties in England, getting out and about, probing the past. But for a young woman like you –'

'Young woman? How old do you think I am?'

He groaned inwardly. He was bound to get this wrong. Cautiously, he cast a quick glance at her, noting the flawless perfection of her skin, and said, 'Maybe twenty-six –'

'And the rest!' she snorted. 'I won't see thirty-two again. But that's the problem you Westerners have, isn't it? You always think Chinese women look younger than they are.'

'Do you see yourself as Chinese?' he asked curiously.

'No. Certainly not culturally, after the time I've spent in England. And yet with a Scottish father, not English either. And Singapore is a long way away, in all senses. So I'm not sure I know how I see myself – other than as an archaeologist.' She paused and was silent for a little while, apparently enjoying the countryside they passed through. 'So what's the story with you and Karen Stannard?' she asked suddenly.

'Story? How do you mean?' Arnold asked defensively.

'Well, it's clear there's a problem of some kind. Is it because you were there in the department before her? How long have you been there anyway?'

Arnold shrugged. 'A few years. I worked in the Planning Department for a while, before I moved.'

She laughed. 'Yes, I gather you gained a reputation there for being somewhat awkward.'

'I wouldn't say that.' He was a little nettled. 'There were a few difficulties, I'll admit . . . but I was glad to make the move. As for there being a problem with Miss Stannard, I think you shouldn't pay too much attention to office gossip.'

'There's plenty of that.'

He glanced sideways at her. 'You've obviously met Jerry Picton.'

'God, yes! Those green teeth!'

Arnold laughed. Picton was notorious for his retailing of gossip, some of it ill-informed, most of it malicious. 'He'll certainly have made some comments.'

'He has. But I've made my own observations too, in the short time I've been working in the department. She was trying to needle you, over my appointment, of course. But I also get the impression she doesn't trust you. Why is that?'

Portia Tyrrel was very direct, Arnold realised. 'I wouldn't know. You'd have to ask her.'

'Strange ... It's all somewhat ambiguous, you know? She seems very wary of you, concerned to know what you're doing, what you may be thinking. You've a good reputation in the department, and out of it.'

'I'm not so certain about that.'

'I am. I'd heard of you before I joined the department. You were the one who found the *sudarium* now on display in the British Museum; then there was the Romano-Celtic burial at Garrigill, and the Viking sword *Kvernbitr* –'

'There were others involved in all that.'

'Yes, but even so ... You've *done* things, made yourself a reputation. And there's no doubt Miss Stannard respects you, perhaps even admires you. But at the same time she's so very careful about you. Watchful. And my appointment ... I suspect an attempt to put you in your place, as she sees it. So, what's it about? Professional jealousy?'

'She has no need for that sort of nonsense. She's an academic; a professional in her own right, with a track record of her own. I think you're seeing things that aren't there,' Arnold replied uncomfortably.

'Maybe. But others have commented ... At the same time, as I said, there's something *ambiguous* about her attitude towards you ... I know you're not married. Have you got a girlfriend?'

It was time to end this conversation. 'We'll be in Warkworth in a few minutes,' he said firmly.

She exclaimed in delight as they passed the castle itself,

perched high on a naturally strong position above the loop of the Coquet. The road dropped ahead of them into Warkworth village, still medieval in appearance and layout. 'It was established as a borough in the twelfth century,' Arnold explained, 'but the present houses are mainly eighteenth- and nineteenth-century. Still, you can see the old burgage plots flanking the street, and at the far end of the village there's the old bridge – it's defended by a gatehouse and it's one of the few fortified bridges in Britain.'

'It's beautiful,' she exclaimed and Arnold nodded, grateful to have manoeuvred her away from the earlier conversation.

'I think Colonel McArdle will be expecting us at the hotel there on the left. And it looks as though there's no problem parking.'

They parked, and entered the hotel to be greeted in the reception area by a small, fussy faded woman in a floral print dress. She gushed at them, introducing herself as Miss Lawrence and explaining that the committee members were in the lounge, that Colonel McArdle was already there to meet them, and that the members of the society would be expected to begin arriving in perhaps half an hour's time. Meanwhile, they could all take tea together: wouldn't that be nice? And she was so *grateful* that Mr Landon had found time to come and address them today. She was certain that his account of the palisaded settlements in Northumberland would be absolutely *fascinating*.

Colonel McArdle was indeed waiting in the lounge with a small coterie of women and one other man, elderly and somewhat infirm-looking. McArdle himself was of middle height and military bearing, stocky, robust of manner and positive of demeanour. He had lost most of his hair; what remained was a strip of sandy fuzz above his ears, but his eyes were hard and his jaw pugnacious. He was dressed in a dark blue blazer with a regimental badge, crisp white shirt and regimental tie, and sharply creased grey flannels. He stood with his back to the fireplace, his legs braced apart as though prepared to ward off sudden attack, and when he shook hands with Arnold the grip was fierce, almost competitive. 'So,' he barked, 'you've just come down from Alnwick, hey? Know it well: I was located there, you know, in my last posting. Based at the Abbot's Tower – regi-

51

mental museum of the Royal Northumberland Fusiliers. Bit different from Northern Ireland, I can tell you – did a stint there. Missed the Gulf, of course, but that's the penalty of getting old, isn't that so?'

He was in his late fifties, Arnold guessed, but he had kept himself trim and fit: no doubt he would be active among the shooting and fishing fraternity in the county. And Arnold seemed to remember hearing that McArdle was also involved as a foot-follower of one of the local packs of beagles.

'Anyway, glad you could make it,' McArdle was saying. He glanced appraisingly, and with clear approval, at Portia Tyrell. 'And this is your secretary?'

She smiled sweetly, with no hint of remonstrance. 'No, actually I'm assistant to Miss Stannard.'

'Ah, my apologies. As a lonely old widower I had of course been looking forward to seeing Miss Stannard again – lovely woman – but I am in no way disappointed that she's not shown up, now that I've had the opportunity to meet you, Miss Tyrel.' He bowed gallantly as he spoke, took her hand and bent over it, brushing it with his lips. Over the shining crown of his head, she looked at Arnold and raised her eyebrows, rolling her eyes expressively.

'Anyway,' McArdle continued in a patronising tone, 'if you'd like to go along with Miss Lawrence and meet the members of the committee, Miss Tyrrel, perhaps Mr Landon and I could have a word together for a moment? You'll excuse us, I'm sure.'

He led Arnold to one side and gestured towards the bar. 'It'll be quieter in there – and more amenable. We've got a while before the audience turns up. There won't be all that many; not more than twenty I'd say. The topic of the lecture doesn't exactly grab one, does it, hey?'

Arnold smiled as the colonel led the way into the bar. Like Portia Tyrrel, the colonel believed in directness. 'Gin?' the colonel called over his shoulder.

'A half of lager will do.'

'Of course. Driving. Still . . .' He placed the orders, waited until the glasses arrived and then said, 'Let's take that table over there in the corner.' Armed with a gin and tonic and a lager the colonel led the way, taking the captain's chair and allowing Arnold to slide into the bench seat opposite him. 'Cheers.'

Arnold acknowledged the greeting and sipped his drink. The colonel leaned forward, elbows on the table between them. 'I suppose Karen Stannard briefed you about the trouble I'm getting.'

'I beg your pardon?'

'I'd hoped she'd be coming up here herself ... damned fine-looking woman, you know ... so that we could have a face-to-face chat about things. She's not been able to give me an appointment, and things are getting out of hand. I've sent several letters of course, and they'll be on file.'

Arnold shook his head. 'I'm sorry. She asked me to stand in for her today, to speak to the society, but I'm afraid she gave me no briefing on any ... problems you might be facing.'

'*Might* be?' McArdle snorted. 'No might about it. So she hasn't told you about Deerbolt Hall, or the Ridgeway estate problem?'

Arnold shook his head.

McArdle frowned. He took a hefty pull at his gin and tonic and regarded the half-empty glass gloomily. 'That's a damned shame. I'd hoped ... You know I live up at Riggs Manor?'

Arnold nodded. He knew the house. There had originally been a castle on the hill at Riggs but it had been destroyed in the fourteenth century and the stone robbed, so that little remained now at its original location, other than jumbled piles of overgrown masonry. At some stage, however, an unfortified stone house had been built close by, maybe as part of the castle development, and in succeeding centuries it had been improved and added to until it came to be regarded as a fine example of an eighteenth-century gentleman's residence, overlooking a considerable acreage of farmland. Colonel McArdle had bought it and moved in three years ago, Arnold gathered: it no longer possessed the acreage, of course, but it made for a comfortable and impressive home. One that probably accorded with McArdle's view of himself as a retired army officer, and pillar of the community.

'Well, I've been getting problems with the adjoining property – the Ridgeway inheritance. Their boundaries are unclear, and

I've got no satisfaction from the damned lawyers, but I know my rights. I've had the odd contretemps with that bloody estate manager they've got – name of Carter, arrogant bastard – and I've written to that young whippersnapper who spends most of his time in London ... and you know all about *him*, I've no doubt.' The colonel snorted contemptuously. 'Drugs and drink and too much damned cash at his disposal. It's an old story, isn't that so? Over-indulgent parents, absent when their presence is most needed ...'

Arnold shook his head. 'I don't think I know the family ... or the nature of your problem.'

McArdle regarded him coldly for a few moments. 'Problems, really. Deerbolt isn't exactly *my* problem, but it's a matter of principle as far as I'm concerned. Look here, there isn't time to go into all this right now. Dinner?'

Startled, Arnold hesitated. 'I'm not sure –'

'Intended asking Miss Stannard up to Riggs, of course.' The colonel's eyes glittered. 'Would have been a sort of tête-à-tête, if you know what I mean. So I'd arranged the necessary catering and all that. Since you're here, and don't know about what I'm facing, you'd better come to dinner tonight. After the talk to the society.' He drained his gin and tonic and rose, to get himself another. 'And you'd better bring that little popsy with you as well. Pretty little thing, ain't she?'

McArdle had been right in his prediction about numbers: just nineteen people turned up to join the committee in the hotel conference room for the talk. They all settled down with the friendly murmurings that might be expected of a group of elderly people who regarded their membership of the society as much as a social as an educational matter, and they began with wide eyes and expectant faces. It was not long however before one or two of them began to droop: eyes grew heavy and chins dropped as Arnold spoke of the days when the stone-built hillforts of Northumberland were a protective necessity. He talked about the plethora of Iron Age farmsteads to be found in the north-east as against the distinct lack of them westwards, and concentrated on the palisaded settlements, describing the homesteads at High Knowes and Humbleton Hill hillfort.

To be fair to the chairman of the antiquarian society, he stuck it out well: of course, as a military man McArdle would be expected to have some interest in citadel-type hillforts established on commanding fell crests. But Arnold was relieved when there were no questions – other than two from the still-gushing Miss Lawrence – and a vote of thanks was called for.

'I enjoyed it anyway,' Portia Tyrrel confided in him half an hour later, when they took their leave and prepared to follow Colonel McArdle in his Land Rover to dinner at Riggs Manor.

Arnold guessed she was just being tactful: he had few illusions about his skills as a public speaker. He kept the colonel's Land Rover in sight as they drove out of Warkworth and northwards towards Rothbury, following the line of the Coquet. After a while the Land Rover swung left towards the village of Riggs and they proceeded along narrow lanes with high-sided banks, ancient hollows that would have been laid down in Saxon times as farm and land boundaries, but which had also served as trackways. They finally emerged just east of Riggs and began to climb the hill on a single stone track that gave them splendid views to the left and right as they rose. A final descent across a ford that was running surprisingly high, and they reached the imposing façade of Riggs Manor.

'A beautiful house,' Portia murmured.

Arnold nodded. 'It's a complete three-storeyed house. Originally there would have been a barn-like building comprising a medieval hall; the hall would later have been screened, and then later still a series of store-rooms added which in time were converted into "parlours" –'

'That's the French designation which in English was translated as "bowers", from *burh*, meaning a stronghold of privacy for the householder,' Portia interrupted him.

Arnold laughed. 'Forgive me, I tend to lecture as though I'm speaking to the ignorant.'

'As someone whose specialism is the Romano-Celtic period I *am* largely ignorant on the matter of medieval houses,' she confessed. 'But this kind of house has always fascinated me. Look at the bell tower – so incongruous, and yet such a feature!'

'Nineteenth-century,' Arnold remarked drily. 'And quite out of keeping with the general plan of the house.'

McArdle waited for them at the steps leading up to the main entrance. He was clearly proud of his possession and he pointed out to them the massive, iron-studded doors – 'Also nineteenth-century,' Arnold whispered to Portia – and the picture gallery that had been built at the far end of what was left of the original, great medieval hall.

'The caterers are at work in the kitchens,' McArdle explained. 'Can't afford permanent staff these days of course, other than a couple of part-time gardeners, and some cleaners who come in from Riggs . . . not like it used to be in the old days. But a drink in my study and then I'll give you a tour of the house before we dine.'

The tour was instructive. Arnold had visited the house some years before but only briefly: now, he was able to take in with pleasure the Tudor wall-fireplace with its carved escutcheon from a long-forgotten family; Flemish brick which suggested a period of wealthy sheep-farming and proud consumerism; a Renaissance oriel window which gave a narrow view of a side alley, a fennel passing along the flank of the house and giving access to the rear. Riggs Manor presented a charming hodge-podge of styles but Arnold liked it – it provided evidence of the development of English architecture, and bore witness to the changing, individual tastes of a series of owners who had lived here at the old house.

'But this is what I like best of all,' McArdle announced as he opened the narrow wooden door and began the ascent up the spiralled stone stairs into the bell tower. 'I like to think that men have come up here for hundreds of years to view their land-holdings.'

Arnold had no desire to disillusion him. The stairs were old, certainly, but would originally have led to a store-room, not a bell tower. But he could take McArdle's point when they finally stepped out on to the square, stoned area under the cupola of red stone. 'No bell now, of course,' the colonel said, 'but look at the view.'

'Magnificent,' Portia Tyrrel breathed.

They leaned against the crenellated parapets and looked around them. From this height they could look eastwards to the sea and note how the swings and loops formed by the Coquet as it made its way to the sea glistened in the dying sun. They were on a plateau which extended to the west and there were views of sweeping farmland, dark copses and spinneys, distant blue hillscapes fading into the skyline. 'Out there, that's the Ridgeway estate,' McArdle explained. 'Sheep farming, mainly, and while I've got no problem with that, there's the damned stock fence that's been broken again. It's my contention, you see, that the line of the estate should not be there at all. My deeds clearly show a mapping of the area, and there's some twenty metres of my land that's been encroached upon. That damned man Carter argues that he's merely following orders and land fences that have been there for generations. I don't care about that: my deeds are explicit.'

'Is that the issue you've raised with our department?' Arnold asked. 'Because if that is the case, I'm afraid it's not in our province to deal with it.'

'I'm aware you can't *adjudicate* on the matter,' McArdle said somewhat testily. 'In the end I think it'll be a matter for the courts because I'm getting no satisfaction from the owners. But I've been writing to Karen Stannard to ask for assistance in identifying the line of the estate boundaries. Your department will have access to old maps that seem to be missing from county archives. Your Museums section would seem to have collected most of the old tithe maps, and I merely want information.'

Arnold could guess that Karen Stannard might not want to get the department involved in land disputes: it was not exactly within their brief. He remained silent, and looked out over the rolling farmland.

'What's that splendid building over there, on the skyline?' Portia asked, breaking the awkward silence that had developed.

McArdle grunted unpleasantly. 'That's the location of the other issue that I've been writing to your department about, and one that you probably won't be able to shrug off responsibility for. That, Miss Tyrrel, is Deerbolt Hall, and the scene of much shenanigans, in my view.' He turned away, and clumped back towards the stairs. 'I'll tell you all about *that* particular matter over dinner.'

57

2

Detective Chief Inspector Culpeper groaned aloud. He eyed his *bête noire*, Inspector Farnsby, with distaste. It was not that he was riven with resentment that Farnsby had a graduate background, was quick and perceptive and keen; nor was it that he was niggled that the Chief Constable clearly held Farnsby in high regard; it wasn't even that there was a marked contrast between the two men – Farnsby with his lean, saturnine features and washed-out blue eyes, and Culpeper with his dinosaurian attitudes to the job, thick-waisted, grey-haired, discontented and edging towards retirement. It was just that he didn't *like* Farnsby.

'So what is it this time?' he asked in a disgruntled tone.

'A liaison job. Down at York. I didn't ask for this, sir –'

'But it still means reorganising work schedules and case files. I suppose it's the Chief has asked for you again.'

'It's an Interpol matter. There's a group being formed to look into the disappearance of some American who might have been involved in the drugs trade in Spain. He was last traced on a flight from Valencia to Newcastle, and it looks as though my job is going to be to co-ordinate the hunt as far as Northumberland is concerned.'

'Seems a bit vague to me,' Culpeper grumbled. ' "Might have been involved" . . . I mean, what specifically have they got on this villain?'

'I won't have the full picture until I meet the other officers concerned with the matter. But I gather it has something to do with the corpse they fished out of the sea some time back, off Robin Hood's Bay.'

'Don't recall it. Nothing to do with us anyway. I can't understand what the Chief's about, sending personnel off on wild-goose chases like that, when our own work load is so bloody heavy . . .' Culpeper sighed, eyeing the thick wad of manila files Farnsby was carrying. 'All right, better hand them over.'

Farnsby placed the files on Culpeper's desk. 'I've tagged a couple of these, suggesting who they might be handled by. There's some routine stuff there, which can be picked up by Davis and Todworthy –'

'And other stuff which will land on *my* desk,' Culpeper interrupted sourly. 'All right. You want to give me a pointer on anything urgent?'

Farnsby hesitated, his pale eyes wary. He selected the top file and placed it in front of Culpeper. 'There is this one. I think you'd better deal with it fairly quickly.'

Culpeper scowled at the name on the file. 'Colin Ledbury?' The name jangled in his memory. 'He's known to us?'

'A local family,' Farnsby said carefully.

There was something in his tone which made Culpeper frown suspiciously. 'Gentry?'

Farnsby nodded.

Culpeper sighed. 'And the Chief Constable thinks it should be given priority. Bloody county connections . . .' He shook his head dolefully. 'So what is it this time? We have to handle it with kid gloves? Keep things under wraps? Make special arrangements?'

Farnsby grimaced. 'It's a bit more delicate than that. Colin Ledbury . . . well, he has a record, as you'll see from the file.'

Culpeper opened the folder and read the summary sheet quickly. Colin Ledbury, twenty-six years old, expelled from public school for smoking cannabis, picked up and charged in London with theft, community service orders, charged with assault with a deadly weapon and acquitted, then served a one-year sentence for possession . . . 'Busy little lad,' Culpeper mused. 'But all these offences were committed outside our manor. North London, Westminster . . . Has he been up to something up here?'

Farnsby shrugged. 'Not so far as we know. But his father died recently, and it seems he came north for the funeral, then set off south again. Now he's back, and he's been in to see the Chief, who got this file raised.'

'With what objective?' Culpeper wondered. 'And why is it to be treated urgently?'

Farnsby hesitated. 'Because Ledbury's here.'

59

'Where?'

'Here at headquarters. Now. He wants to talk to someone senior. And the Chief says it can't be me because I have to go to York.'

'So it has to be *me*.' Culpeper shook his head mournfully. 'So what's it all about? Have I got to read him the riot act? Tell him we don't want him playing around with dangerous substances here in Northumberland? Or do I just hold his hand and tell him not to be a naughty boy?'

'I don't think that's quite it, sir. He came in to see *us*. To register a complaint.'

Culpeper snorted. 'Police brutality, I suppose. Given the chance, I'd wring his bloody little privileged public school neck . . .' He glowered. 'You went to public school, didn't you?'

'Yes, sir.'

The woodenness of the reply did not escape Culpeper. He snapped the file closed and leaned back in his chair. 'Well, if Mr Ledbury is here, and wants to be interviewed, and the Chief wants it to be given some priority, that's exactly what I'd better do, isn't it? All right, Farnsby, be my dogsbody for once. Send the whippersnapper in and I'll see what's troubling the poor lad.'

As Farnsby reached the door, Culpeper added, 'And have a nice time in York.'

Colin Ledbury introduced himself as soon as he came in through the door but he was not alone: he was accompanied by a broad-shouldered man with dark hair and leathery features. There was something nervous about the man's eyes: they never seemed to be still, but were constantly shifting as though seeking the main chance. His skin was marked along one cheek, as though he had been burned at some time and the consequent skin graft had not been entirely successful. He sat a little behind Ledbury: watchful, ill at ease but controlled.

Ledbury himself was tall, fair hair cut short, a little pudgy around the jowls, with designer stubble on his chin. His grey eyes were watchful and suspicious. He appeared to be bursting to say something, so Culpeper ignored him for a moment and stared at his companion.

'And you are . . .?'

'My name's Carter.'

The voice was deep, the tone surly, and he avoided Culpeper's glance, staring down at thick, twisting hands. Culpeper frowned: there was something familiar about the man. 'Have we met before?' he asked.

Carter shrugged but made no reply. Culpeper waited a little while, thinking. He had come across Carter before, and in a professional capacity, too. It was something to do with South Shields, but he could not quite put his finger on it.

Colin Ledbury was not prepared to allow Culpeper time to think about it. 'Whether you know Carter or not is irrelevant,' he snapped in an irritated voice. 'We're here –'

'Yes,' Culpeper interrupted him ponderously, 'you're here to register some sort of complaint, I understand. Now perhaps we'd better begin by going through some formalities. Mr Ledbury, you reside at . . .?'

'I live in London,' Ledbury replied, reddening with anger. 'But I'm not here –'

'Address?' Culpeper required pleasantly, but firmly.

He wrote down the address Ledbury gave him, noting the suppressed fury in the man's tone. 'And Mr Carter?'

'He's just here to –' Ledbury stopped, glaring at the raised eyebrows in front of him. He took a deep breath and controlled himself. 'Carter works for . . . works for the estate of my late father. Estate manager, and he lives in a cottage on the estate.'

'And he's connected with the . . . complaint you want to make?' Culpeper asked with exaggerated care. 'Or is he just along with you to provide *support* of some kind?'

The contemptuous suggestion of hand-holding led to a short silence as Ledbury glared furiously at Culpeper, but he managed to control his temper. It was clear he was not used to being treated in this manner, but there was something in Culpeper that he found intimidating.

'I asked Carter to come along, because I'm aware how you people work. I –'

'Yes, I understand you have some familiarity with police procedures,' Culpeper interrupted amiably.

Ledbury's grey eyes were cold. 'I knew that you would want first-hand evidence, rather than just my word for things,' he

61

went on. 'And rather than give you all further excuses for time-wasting, I thought it would be a good idea to have Carter here when I registered my complaint with the Chief Constable.'

'Ah, yes, the Chief Constable. Friend of yours, Mr Ledbury?'

'He knew my father,' Ledbury gritted.

Culpeper smiled unpleasantly. 'Of course. *Your* social scene has been in the London area, I understand, so you won't have got to know this force very well. But we have heard of you, of course . . .'

There was a short silence. Both men sat still, staring at Culpeper, who was aware of a growing animosity towards him. It cheered him somewhat, making up for his annoyance at the redeployment of Inspector Farnsby.

'Shall we get on with the reason for my presence here?' Ledbury said at last, in an icy tone.

'Why not?' Culpeper replied cheerily, feeling everyone in the room now had things in a proper perspective. 'Now exactly what is the substance of your complaint?'

Ledbury sat up a little straighter. 'It's a week or more since my sister went missing and nothing's been done about it. Indeed, the whole matter doesn't seem to have been taken at all seriously.'

Culpeper raised his eyebrows. 'Your sister . . .' He consulted the contents of the file in front of him, while the silence grew heavy in the room. 'Grace Ledbury . . . Ah, yes. A week ago, you say . . . ten days, actually . . . I note that your sister is thirty years of age.'

'That's right. I don't see what that has to do with –'

'Well, of course, if she had been a child we would have acted urgently. If she had been a teenager, we might have been concerned. But when a mature woman perhaps decides to take a holiday, she doesn't have to tell us, or her brother either, I would think, if he's living in London –'

'It's not like her,' Ledbury snapped.

'How would you know?' Culpeper asked mildly. 'As far as I can gather you've been living in London since you were seventeen and according to what I read here you've not apparently spent much time in the north at all.'

'I don't have to take this,' Ledbury snarled. 'The disappearance of my sister has been reported, but no one seems at all concerned. If I don't get satisfaction –'

'What would give you satisfaction, Mr Ledbury? Why are you so concerned? Do you have any suspicions concerning what the papers call *foul play?*'

As he used the words a brief flashing thought came to him, concerning the heavy man seated just behind Ledbury. He glanced at him; the man's eyes darted away and he seemed momentarily disconcerted. 'For the sake of the record,' Culpeper continued, smiling thoughtfully, 'maybe you'd better start at the beginning.'

'The last time I saw my sister,' Ledbury explained harshly, 'was when I came north for my father's funeral. I only stayed a few days and then returned to London.'

'You parted on amicable terms?' Culpeper asked.

'Of course,' Ledbury snapped. 'We haven't fallen out in any way. Though what that's got to do ... Anyway, about ten days ago Carter phoned me. I'd been trying to get in touch with Grace for some time but she never seemed to be around. On the phone Carter told me he hadn't seen my sister for several days. She seemed to be missing. I immediately came north. And then I asked the police to look for her. Nothing happened –'

'Hold on,' Culpeper said, raising a hand. He fixed his glance on Carter. 'Let's get things a bit more clear. You live on the estate. You hadn't seen Grace Ledbury. But were you accustomed to seeing her often?'

Carter hesitated. He lifted a reluctant shoulder. 'I can't say I've seen her often. I mean, she wasn't living on the estate when her father was alive: she had some sort of job in Harrogate, I believe. But she gave that up when her father died and she came to live at Ridgeway Hall.'

'But that's a matter of ... what ... months? And she was accustomed to consulting you, seeing you regularly once she moved in?'

Carter reddened somewhat. 'No, of course not. I met her a couple of times, when she asked me questions about the estate.'

'She's a mature woman, of independent means, she'd been working in Harrogate, she has friends there, I imagine ... she wouldn't necessarily have to tell you where she was going, Mr Carter?'

'Of course not! But I was told that Mr Ledbury had been ringing, there was no sign of Miss Ledbury at the Hall, no one seemed to know where she had gone, so I rang him, told him she had disappeared.'

'I see. Helpful of you.' Culpeper stared at the man for a little while, casting his mind back. Something about South Shields . . . He turned to Ledbury. 'You say you'd been trying to contact your sister. Was there any particular reason why you'd been trying to get hold of her?'

For a moment Ledbury seemed unwilling to reply. Then he said, 'It was family business. I wanted to talk to her. It has no bearing on –'

South Shields. A beating in the car-park of a local pub. A man called Archer. Culpeper shifted his gaze back to Carter. Of course, that was it. Archer had been known as a member of an enforcement mob at Shields, working for a gambling syndicate. Quite what he had been doing at the pub that time was never substantiated, but there had been an altercation of sorts, and Archer had been set upon in the pub car-park. Carter had been arrested, charges of grievous bodily harm had been brought but the matter had never come to trial. It was well enough understood among the police that pressure had been brought to bear upon the few witnesses present. But all this had been ten years ago . . . Carter had dropped out of the Tyneside scene, moved on – and upwards, it seemed – since then. Ten years ago he had been on the fringe of the protection rackets on Tyneside. Now, somehow, he had managed to become an estate manager . . . Culpeper's glance came back to Ledbury. He wondered whether it was this young man who had helped Carter take his step up to seeming respectability. And if so, why he would have done it.

Culpeper grunted. 'It may well have no bearing on the case. Unless, of course, you'd been bothering your sister in some way. Maybe she didn't want to see you –'

'Why should that be?' Ledbury demanded harshly. 'She's my sister –'

'I've got some information on the file here,' Culpeper interrupted cheerily. 'When your father died, he left quite a bit of money, tied up mainly in the estate, of course.'

There was a short silence. Ledbury's eyes glittered. 'So?'

'He left the bulk of his estate to his daughter . . . apart from certain legacies to charity and so on. And the Hunt. But you . . . I gather there was little or no mention of you. From what we've got on this file, you seem to have been largely . . . forgotten.'

Ledbury's mouth was hard. 'I don't see what right you've got to go prying into my family affairs –'

'Oh, it's just that I've got a very efficient inspector here at headquarters who likes to get all his facts straight,' Culpeper reassured him. 'Me, I wouldn't have bothered, but when Inspector Farnsby was asked to start looking into your sister's disappearance he decided to get everything he could that was of public record. I mean, your father's will was *published*, of course.'

'The fact that my father left me nothing in his will is irrelevant,' Ledbury blustered. 'When Carter told me she was missing I became concerned. I came north to look for her. And I came here for assistance. All I'm getting is delay and insinuation and –'

'Insinuation?' Culpeper interrupted, raising his thick eyebrows in mock surprise. 'I don't know what you mean. I'm sure it's brotherly love that brings you north from your . . . activities down south. As for delays . . . we're looking into the matter, but Grace Ledbury's *disappearance* cannot yet give us cause for concern. She could have slipped across to America for a holiday, or Spain, or the Seychelles; she could have gone to France on a booze run; she could have decided to drop out of sight for a while. She could even be trying to avoid people who have been sending her begging letters, since she came into her inheritance . . . Or maybe she's run off with an Italian count. Who can tell? We'll pursue enquiries, because you're clearly concerned. But as I said before . . . she's a lady of full age, and if she wants to go walkabout, that's her privilege. So, as I said before, unless you've got some reason to suspect foul play . . .'

Ledbury got to his feet angrily. Carter rose with him, more slowly. Ledbury's mouth twisted unpleasantly as he glared at Culpeper. 'I can see I'd be getting nowhere relying on you! My

65

sister's disappeared but there's no way you're going to take this seriously! If there's anything to be done, I'm going to have to do it myself!'

His anger was real, but Culpeper noted that it seemed to contain a hint of panic.

Two days later Culpeper met the Chief Constable in the car-park of headquarters at Ponteland. The Chief Constable was just getting into his chauffeured car when he saw Culpeper. He beckoned him over. 'This Ledbury affair.'

'Sir?'

'What do you make of it?'

Culpeper shrugged. 'We've no reports, sir, and Miss Ledbury can go wandering if she wishes . . .'

'Humph . . .' The Chief Constable looked unhappy. He shook his head. 'There's questions being asked . . . And young Ledbury, he's a bad 'un. We need to go carefully with that one. Watch our backs, you know what I mean?'

'No, sir, I don't.'

The Chief Constable seemed uncomfortable. 'It may well be he's been trying to get money out of his sister. Nothing confirmed, of course, but I hear on the grapevine that since he was cut out of his father's will, he's been making a bit of a nuisance of himself. It could be he's got into trouble down south, and has wanted bailing out.' He wrinkled his nose in distaste. 'Now, we don't want any trouble, and we don't want any more family scandal about the Ledburys emerging. If we can keep that young man down south without any more noise up here, everyone will be happy. Myself included. So, do your best, Culpeper . . . but no more noise than is necessary, you understand?'

Culpeper understood. The county did not like to have its scions, tearaways though they might be, held up to contumely in the Press. So, he was supposed to find out where Miss Ledbury had got to, but quietly . . .

3

On the way to his departmental conference with Karen Stannard, Arnold stopped off at the Planning Department. Several of the people working there nodded to him: they knew him well enough from the days when he had worked in the department himself, though he had formed no firm friendships among them. The most senior man there now was Fred Orrell, a grizzly Cumbrian who had retained his accent and slowness of speech: sometimes Arnold had felt that talking to Fred was almost like phoning someone in Australia – there was occasionally a gap of a couple of seconds as though response times were affected by a distance between them. But he liked Fred Orrell: the man was genuine and honest. And he kept his ear to the ground.

'Long time, no see, Arnold. How are things? Miss Stannard keeping you in check?'

'Like always,' Arnold smiled.

'Coffee?'

'I'm on my way to a meeting; it'll make me late, but what the hell!'

'Not like the old Arnold! You must be looking for another job, or something.'

Arnold grunted. These days, the Mojave desert was never far from his mind.

'I said coffee, but it's more like sludge,' Orrell grumbled as he brought a plastic cup across for Arnold from the machine in the corridor. 'So, what brings you into this department again? We don't see much of you since you got translated.'

'Bit of information, really,' Arnold replied, sipping his coffee. He grimaced. Orrell was right: it did taste of something akin to mud. 'You come across a character called Colonel McArdle?'

'Ahah! The owner of Riggs Manor.' Fred Orrell leaned back in his chair, cupping his coffee in two hands. 'Aye, we have the occasional run in with the colonel. Since he's been living up at Riggs he's almost never off the phone.'

'Planning problems?'

Orrell digested the thought. 'More than one. Pesters us for plans, wants to know what estate deeds we've got, keeps asking us for information about other properties and landholdings. Some of the time I think his requests would be better dealt with by your department.'

'Antiquarian stuff? Yes, he chairs a local antiquarian society,' Arnold replied.

'Aye. But we do what we can.'

'What about Riggs Manor itself?'

'Why do you ask?' Orrell queried after a thoughtful silence.

'I've been up there,' Arnold replied. 'He raised with me some kind of dispute he's having with the Ridgeway estate. Wanted us to do something about it, but I thought I'd warn you that I suggested it should really lie with your people.'

Fred Orrell sighed. 'Ridgeway, aye ... No need to give me warning. He's been on to us several times. And if you ask me, it's all going to end in tears.'

'How do you mean?'

Orrell sucked at his teeth and gazed at his coffee cup. He seemed unhappy. 'The colonel's all right, I suppose. But snappy, bit sharp, wants things done yesterday. If he's got a land dispute with Ridgeway Hall, there's not much we can do about it. Lawyers need to be called in. But McArdle, well, he's a bit bull at the gate, you know? And he's had a few clashes with the staff at Ridgeway. Particularly with a man called Carter. Not a nice man.'

'He did mention something about it.'

Orrell shook his head. 'Don't know where Carter came from. But he's a rough character. Came in here once, and I didn't like the look of him. Got a nasty eye on him. How he pulled the job I don't know; old man Ledbury was pretty senile towards the end, and left the running of the place to some rather odd people, if you ask me. After he died, there was a bit of a clear-out as far as staff were concerned, and then Carter was brought in as estate manager. Not long after that there was talk about selling off some of the land for development purposes, quite close to the McArdle boundary line in fact, but we never saw an application here in the department ... and as for Carter, well, he's a bit hands-on, in the modern idiom. And he takes things personally – had a few clashes with McArdle about those boundaries. Not far off physical, if you know what I mean.'

'They came to blows?'

'Near enough, I hear.' Orrell finished his coffee and tossed the plastic cup into a waste basket. 'Only last week they were trading insults again. And McArdle's got a hot temper. He'd better be careful of dark nights with Carter, though . . .'

'Well, I thought I'd better mention it to you. Boundary disputes aren't really our business.'

'Nor ours, when they get this nasty. All over a few metres . . .' Orrell shook his head sadly. 'Anyway, we've given McArdle all he's asked for, within our own records. But in the end it'll have to go to court . . . if Carter lets it get that far without belting the colonel where it hurts.'

'Where does the owner stand in all this?' Arnold asked curiously.

Fred Orrell considered the matter. 'Old man Ledbury died last year. There was some delay settling the inheritance, and that's when there was talk of building developments – to settle outstanding estate debts, I imagine. But it died down again.'

'So who owns the Ridgeway estate now?' Arnold asked.

Orrell shrugged. 'I think there were two children . . . everything seems to have gone to the daughter. And that didn't please her brother too much, so the gossip says. But, none of our business . . . As for where the daughter stands in the dispute, her name has just never been raised. She didn't live with her father – neither her nor her brother. There'd been some kind of falling out. She only moved in some months after his death. And Carter and McArdle, well, it's no skin off Carter's nose, of course, but I got the impression he's the kind of man who always likes to get into a fight . . . and doesn't give way very easily. Particularly towards a stuffed shirt like Colonel McArdle. I mean . . . he does tend to sort of stand on his rights, don't he?'

Karen Stannard was waiting in her office when Arnold finally arrived. So was Portia Tyrrel. There was something in the atmosphere that made Arnold feel they might have been talking about him, but once he had settled himself into a chair Karen Stannard immediately attended to business, after a short, sharp comment about his timekeeping: she started reviewing the work situation, asking questions about progress on the various sites being supervised by Arnold, and putting Portia in the picture as far as some of the outstanding issues were concerned. She explained to them both about her own diary and amendments that would have to be made to Arnold's schedules and she suggested the transfer of certain responsibilities to Portia Tyrrel. Arnold made no demur.

At last she settled back with a thin smile, her eyes fixed on Arnold. 'That's about it, I think. I'm glad we were able to get through the business so quickly. It would have helped us, Arnold, if you'd got here on time, of course – I'd begun to wonder whether you'd already left us to take up this idyllic offer from the States.' She turned to glance at her assistant. 'Portia and I, we'd begun to panic, not sure what we should do here without you.'

'I called in at the Planning Department,' Arnold explained, ignoring the jibe. 'I thought it a good idea to tell them about Colonel McArdle's boundary dispute.'

'Ah, yes, McArdle . . .' Karen gave a feline smile. 'I understand your . . . talk to his antiquarian society was satisfactory. Sent most of the poor dears to sleep.'

Arnold glanced at Portia. She was sitting very upright, hands demurely placed in her lap, eyes downcast. There was the hint of a smile on her lips. He wondered why she had felt the necessity to tell the acting director about the soporific effect of his talk at Warkworth.

'As for the good colonel,' Karen Stannard was continuing, 'I've already written to him earlier and told him we can't get involved in the matter. But he's a persistent man, isn't he? What's the position in Planning?'

Arnold shrugged. 'They've helped as far as they can, but can't satisfy the colonel. He wants old maps . . .'

'He also wants assistance in another matter,' Portia Tyrrel said. 'Deerbolt Hall.'

Karen Stannard eyed her for a few moments, frowning slightly at the interruption. 'Yes ... Do *you* have thoughts about the matter, Arnold?'

Arnold was suddenly aware of a degree of tension between the two women. Portia Tyrrel was outwardly unmoved, but there was a hint of malice in Karen Stannard's tone. Arnold shrugged. 'Colonel McArdle told us about it over dinner at his home the other evening. Apart from the boundary dispute with the Ridgeway estate, he's also concerned about Deerbolt Hall.'

'On behalf of the antiquarian society,' Portia offered.

Karen ignored her. 'Go on, Arnold. I'd like to hear *your* view.'

Portia's chin came up slightly. Arnold ploughed on. 'It seems that two years ago Deerbolt Hall was sold to some kind of group. Exactly what the group stands for, Colonel McArdle wasn't clear. But he claims to have heard strange sounds –'

'Singing,' Portia said flatly.

'Strange sounds coming from the Hall, and he's seen lights in the woods. He says he doesn't know what's going on, and although it doesn't really affect him personally, as owner of Riggs Manor, being the man he is, he decided to go along and try to find out – the property is just about visible from Riggs Manor. Three weeks ago he went along there and was somewhat alarmed to find there were building contractors' vans parked in the driveway. He tried to get access to the Hall to see the new owners, but was refused entrance. So he spoke to the contractors. According to them, they had been engaged to carry out certain redevelopments to Deerbolt Hall. McArdle wasn't happy about it, so wrote to you –'

'Several times,' Karen Stannard said drily.

'Anyway,' Arnold went on after a short silence, 'the upshot of it all is that McArdle thinks that this group is undertaking work on a building which is listed, and that this should not happen without planning permission. I explained that once again this would be a matter for the appropriate department, but he got a bit niggly at that, talked about buck-passing, and insisted that our department should make the initial investigation, since Deerbolt Hall was also scheduled some years ago for an archaeological investigation –'

'And I tended to agree with him,' Portia said quietly.

'What do *you* think, Arnold?' Karen Stannard asked, a little too sweetly.

Arnold sighed: he was beginning to get the picture as far as the acting director and her assistant were concerned. He shook his head. 'McArdle has a point. He says he's getting nowhere with the Planning people because they say with the backlog they've got, and with local government budgets slashed, they can't get around to it immediately. And they're not even sure there's a problem. They *have* visited once, and found nothing untoward –'

'The colonel says they sent an inexperienced young officer, thinks they were hoodwinked, shown the wrong things,' Portia interrupted.

Karen ignored her; she kept her glance fixed on Arnold as though Portia had not even spoken. 'Be that as it may,' Arnold continued, 'it's difficult to pass judgement. The fact is, the archaeological plans we had are in abeyance for lack of funds –'

'So we have no reason to go in,' Karen mused, 'even though Portia thinks we should insist upon entrance.'

'– but we could use them as an excuse to gain entrance, and sort of generally look around,' Arnold went on. 'If the colonel is right, the situation is dangerous. Deerbolt Hall has never really been investigated properly; if building work is going on there it could damage the fabric, destroy historical traces . . .'

'So, like Portia, you want to go in?'

There was a short silence. Arnold noted that Portia Tyrrel's features were expressionless but she held her body stiffly, as though annoyed about something. He shrugged. 'I think it's worth looking at.'

Karen Stannard sighed dramatically. 'I'm *so* pleased you're able to advise us, Arnold. I wouldn't have wanted to go charging in there without some *senior* advice. Portia rather wanted to take this on as her first real responsibility – in fact, she'd already talked to Councillor Thomson, Chairman of Planning, about it, hadn't you, dear? But I wasn't so sure. I need to take rather more . . . sage counsel. As acting director, I need to be sure that our . . . ah . . . tactics are sound. We don't want to upset anyone, do we?'

Even though Karen had almost made an art form of upsetting people. Arnold waited.

She rose, stretched and walked across to the window; her body was slim, her appearance elegant, and the sunlight gave a faint, reddish tinge to her dark hair. At last she turned and looked full at Arnold, smiling. Her eyes were tawny, satisfied. 'I think the best way forward is to suggest a joint effort. While I have no doubt about Portia's capacity to undertake a suitably low-key study of the matter, experience in Celtic-Romano studies is not perhaps the best background to allow for a proper evaluation of a medieval structure like Deerbolt Hall. And she is rather . . . new to the department, Arnold. I think she . . . *we* would both appreciate it if you were to go along with her on a visit to the Hall. Find out what's going on. Discover whether Planning really do need to have cause for concern. And whether our own department has grounds to worry that the planned archaeological study is likely to be put at risk . . . So shall we handle it like that, then?' The question was rhetorical: she did not even glance at her assistant. 'Good. That's settled.'

Arnold rose, and nodded, gathered up his files and headed for the door. As he reached it, Karen Stannard added, 'And, Arnold, it will sort of take your mind off preoccupations across the Atlantic, won't it?' He looked back, and she smiled at him, raised one eyebrow. 'I take it there's no formal decision taken yet?'

'None,' Arnold said and left.

A few minutes later there was a tap on the door of his office. It was Portia Tyrrel. Her features were composed but there was an angry glint in her eyes. 'I thought we'd better fix some possible dates, for our joint visit to Deerbolt Hall.'

Arnold nodded and reached for his desk diary. As he was checking it, Portia blurted out, 'I'd suggested I take a look at the place myself.'

'I guessed that.'

'Why did she insist that you went along?' Portia's voice had deepened with anger. 'Does she think I can't handle matters myself? The damn thing's simple enough – is there or is there not development going on at Deerbolt Hall. I don't need my hand held in a situation like that!'

Arnold looked up and studied her. She was already beginning

to learn the hard truths about working with Karen Stannard. The acting director was an ambitious, beautiful woman who intended to make the top job hers, permanently. She clearly liked the idea of having an almost equally beautiful woman as her assistant, not least because it gave her support, but also because it was a means of keeping Arnold himself in his place ... *emasculating* him, as she'd said. She'd seen Portia as a useful ally. But Karen Stannard would never lose sight of the danger of having someone close to her who might undermine her in any way. And if Portia Tyrrel was given her head too much, allowed to develop a reputation within the department, that could spell trouble for the acting director. She was wary of Arnold, and would use her assistant to undermine him ... but she would also be wary of Portia.

The director's assistant was staring at Arnold, demandingly. 'Well?'

Arnold shrugged. 'I wouldn't worry too much about it. Miss Stannard's a law unto herself. And you should never assume that you can out-think her, or second-guess her. She is usually – though not always – one jump ahead.'

'*You* seem to know how to handle her,' Portia said slowly.

'No,' Arnold disagreed. 'I just don't make the mistake of underestimating her. And I never tell her things she doesn't really need to know ... even if she *wants* to know them.'

Portia stared at him. She knew what he meant: there had been no need for her to gossip to Karen Stannard about Arnold's talk to the antiquarian society. She had done it, no doubt, to establish some kind of rapport with her boss ... a quiet giggle, two girls together, chattering about the boring talk Arnold Landon had delivered.

But that didn't mean an inside track for Portia Tyrrel – Karen Stannard didn't work like that. She had taken the confidence, but it hadn't affected her judgement when she decided to cut Portia down to size by insisting Arnold work with her at Deerbolt Hall.

'So,' Arnold said cheerfully, 'what about Monday week?'

Sourly, Portia Tyrrel noted it in her diary.

PART THREE

1

Portia was in a better mood when they finally drove to Deerbolt Hall ten days later. She clearly enjoyed escaping from the office, as Arnold did, and she appeared to have forgotten her disappointment at not having the assignment all to herself. Arnold had seen little of her in the interim, since he had been busy on a museum development near Berwick, and he now quite enjoyed her company as she chattered to him on the drive north about Singapore, Asian culture, her research interests and the apartment she had finally managed to acquire just outside Morpeth.

'You live alone, I gather, Arnold?'

'That's right. In Morpeth.'

'But your girlfriend lives in Durham.'

Jerry Picton again, no doubt. Arnold shrugged. 'That's right. But she's been in the States for the last year or so.'

'An author, I gather . . . Is it because she's out there that you're considering going out to work at this desert site?'

Arnold sighed. He wasn't quite sure why he was considering it . . . as he wasn't quite sure why he was hesitating. It was an excellent offer, and an exciting opportunity. When he remained silent, she asked, 'What exactly is the Mojave site all about?'

'It's a shamanistic site. Not all that old by our standards, maybe seven hundred years, but it's somewhat puzzling, in view of the carvings . . .' He went on to explain some of Professor Schwartz's theories.

'Sounds very interesting,' Portia said. 'But you can't make up your mind . . .' She was silent for a little while. 'I get the feeling Karen's somewhat . . . anxious about it all.'

'How do you mean?'

'I don't know. Sometimes I think she'd be glad to see you go. There are other times when I get the feeling she'd, well, miss you somehow . . .'

Like a hole in the head, he thought.

They passed the village of Riggs to their right and as they ascended the wooded hill they caught a glimpse of the bell tower that Colonel McArdle was so proud of. At the crossroads they turned left and soon were proceeding through an avenue of mature beech trees, the carriageway laid down a hundred and fifty years earlier to Deerbolt Hall. When they finally came in sight of the Hall itself, Arnold pulled into the side of the carriageway, his car wheels churning up the soft earth. He reached back to the seat behind him for his briefcase, and drew out the map he had brought with him from the office.

'Right . . . before we go in we'd better have another look at the plans so we make sure we don't miss anything.' He showed the estate plan to Portia, tracing the outlines with his finger.

'Here we are on the carriageway. Now, let's see . . . As far as we've been able to ascertain, the Hall was originally built in the late medieval period as an almshouse. This is borne out by its shape . . . a quadrangular building enclosing a courtyard, around which the inmates had their own apartments. They would eat communally in the great hall, which would have been just here . . . and attached to the hall there would have been the usual domestic offices, like those of a great house –'

'Or even a university college of that period,' Portia suggested.

'That's right. So it followed the typical Carthusian monastic arrangement with the rooms arranged in the normal late-medieval fashion. Access to the courtyard was gained through this gatehouse tower – rather pseudo-military in appearance, really.'

'So where was the area designated for archaeological study by the department?' Portia asked.

Arnold twisted the map so that the layout of the house was more easily appreciated. 'We're here, as I said. Now you'll notice there's a back lane running from the Hall towards the south-east. If you look across there, beyond the house, you'll see that clump of trees . . . yes? That's where this lane runs, and there's a theory that it forms part of a very old Saxon track, or drovers' way, that had fallen into disuse when the almshouse was built. We feel that the rear gate entrance, just there, possibly comprises part of a much older structure, maybe twelfth-century. The thought is that there was probably a farmhouse built there – or maybe even an inn, or perhaps a market of some kind, to which the drovers' track led. So the department decided, when funding was available, that some investigations would be carried out at that external wall, and out towards the drovers' track where there seem to be some old foundations. The question we need to determine is whether, if there is any building work going on at Deerbolt Hall, it's likely to affect that area there.'

'So what's the history of the house?' Portia asked as Arnold put the map back in his briefcase.

'The almshouse was built in the late medieval period but seemed to operate specifically as an almshouse for a relatively short period – maybe not more than twenty years. The buildings had been erected to a monastic plan by Hugh de Vere's mother but he did not seem to have the same feelings for the poor that his mother did. He converted the property pretty quickly after her death. That's why the gatehouse has that military appearance: he fortified it. Anyway, the house remained with the de Veres for two hundred years, then a Sheffield merchant bought it, and it passed through various hands. I've not met the recent owners, and know little about them.'

'Colonel McArdle certainly thinks they're some sort of cult.'

'Colonel McArdle may be right. But that's not really our affair.'

He restarted the engine and drove down the carriageway towards the imposing gateway to Deerbolt Hall.

The gateway itself possessed large, impressive wooden doors of some antiquity, studded with iron rivets. The gate was open, however, and Arnold was able to drive through into the courtyard beyond. Their approach must have been noted, because standing on the steps leading into the main hall at the far end of the courtyard were three women. They were dressed in long grey gowns with crimson sashes at the waist. The gowns were cowled, and the heads of two of the women were covered. The third, who stood slightly ahead of the other two, had thrown back her cowl and was waiting to greet Arnold as he emerged from the car. As he moved towards the steps she held out her hand.

'Good morning. You must be Mr Landon. I am Sister Simone. Welcome to Oclixtan.'

Arnold blinked, and the woman smiled. 'Known to you as Deerbolt Hall.'

Arnold introduced her to Portia and as they shook hands in a formal fashion he observed the woman who had greeted them. Sister Simone was of medium height, perhaps forty years of age, slim, her figure indeterminate under the loose-fitting gown. Her hair was dark, flecked and streaked with wisps of grey and long, drawn back severely to the nape of her neck. Her features were somewhat hawkish, but she was a good-looking woman, he concluded, and one who exuded a mature confidence and ease of manner. Her eyes were deep-set and intelligent, appraising as they glanced back to Arnold. 'Perhaps you would like to come inside. We have coffee awaiting your arrival . . .'

They entered what would have been the great hall of the old almshouse. Its stone walls would have been bare and cold in the old days, but now they had been draped with heavy damask, deep red in colour, so the room was dim and shadowed. Sister Simone led the way with her two companions ranged either side and slightly behind her: Portia glanced at Arnold and raised her eyebrows. She seemed to want to giggle, but that could be nervousness because Arnold himself was aware of a tension in the air, the scent of some kind of incense, a sickly-sweet heaviness in the atmosphere that he found disturbing.

They entered a small room to one side of the great hall: it would originally have been a small chapel, Arnold guessed, for the use of the inmates of the almshouse. Now, well lit by long Norman windows, it held some easy chairs, and a long mahogany table on which had been laid an expensive-looking coffee service. At the far end of the room the stone wall that had probably held a dais or a formal altar had been converted to a fireplace in which a small pile of logs had been laid. It all seemed rather incongruous.

Sister Simone smiled. 'This room is used for the reception of guests. We have not really determined how it should finally be furnished. Coffee?'

The two hooded women silently poured coffee for them and, having shown them to easy chairs, retreated and left the room. Sister Simone sat down facing Arnold and Portia and sipped her coffee. 'We readily agreed to your visit, of course, but we are not entirely clear what it is you want.'

'Are you in charge here?' Arnold asked.

She smiled. 'I am one of the sisters. There is no one ... in charge as you put it. But your interest with us ... Something to do with the history of the building?'

Arnold felt it was important to be frank. 'We had received some reports that you are carrying out some building development −'

'Ah, yes, Colonel McArdle,' she interrupted, with a thin smile. 'He has been here ... A persistent man. But misguided. We have already acceded to a visit from your Planning Department, at his behest − they have declared themselves satisfied that we are committing no ... heinous sins here.' She fixed Arnold with a keen glance, sharp-eyed in her appraisal. 'We have nothing to hide, of course, but we are somewhat puzzled as to why *your* department should now wish to visit us.'

Arnold put down his coffee cup and leaned forward. 'We had reached an arrangement with the previous owners to undertake some archaeological surveys at Deerbolt Hall, mainly to the exterior structure of the building. Lack of finance has prevented us undertaking the work − we merely wished to confirm that it's still possible for us to begin the work, and that it hasn't been affected by any construction activity you're undertaking.'

'I see ...' Sister Simone was silent for a little while. Then she nodded. 'I'm sure we would want to continue to ... co-operate, although we would want to control the access arrangements. We are peaceful here, and the outside world −'

'What exactly is Oclixtan?' Portia Tyrrel interrupted.

Sister Simone looked at her. Her features were grave, her deep-set eyes fixed and intense. 'We are seekers of the second cycle, under our leader.'

Portia injected bafflement into her glance. 'Second cycle? Leader?'

Sister Simone managed a thin smile. 'We are led by David Gilmagesh. We live here in comparative isolation, away from the influences and temptations of the outside world. We have relinquished earthly bonds; we have discarded familial ties; we seek the second cycle which will enable us to see and experience a

81

world that lies beyond the cultural and linguistic constraints of Western rationalism, and which will leave us unencumbered by conditioned conceptions, or by the taint of personal histories.'

'So do I gather that *you* do not own Deerbolt Hall?' Portia asked.

'We reject the normal concept of ownership. David Gilmagesh is our spiritual leader; together we exist in harmony; together we touch our environment and reach beyond it –'

'So Mr . . . Gilmagesh owns Deerbolt,' Portia insisted with a hint of stubbornness.

Irritation briefly touched Sister Simone's brow. It was quickly suppressed. 'This is the abode of Oclixtan. Ownership in your terms is an irrelevance.'

'So how is Oclixtan financed –'

'If you have finished your coffee I can show you what is being done by way of construction,' Sister Simone interrupted imperiously. As she rose, Arnold shot a warning glance in Portia's direction, but she ignored him. Arnold followed as the two women left the room.

Sister Simone led the way back across the courtyard to the gatehouse. She opened the small iron door in the wall and led the way up a winding narrow stone staircase inside the wall to a small crenellated platform above. 'From here you can overlook all of the Hall,' she announced, 'and see what we are doing – and not doing. To begin with, you'll note that nowhere are we attempting to undertake work on the external walls of the property. The only construction work being undertaken is over there, on that roof. It will not be apparent to others, as you shall see shortly . . . The building is of course shaped like a quadrangle. That area over there is sealed – it is the abode of David Gilmagesh. The sisters do not enter there. The rest of the buildings are open to us all, the sisters of Oclixtan, and are where we constantly seek spiritual enlightenment.'

'The sisters of Oclixtan,' Portia muttered. 'How many of you are there?'

'We are eleven. Soon, with the accession of our new submittor, Sister Percepta, we shall be twelve.'

'Submittor?'

Sister Simone smiled gravely, inclining her head. 'She is new to our order: she is presently being initiated into its mysteries.'

'Are there no men here?'

Sister Simone did not answer her. She glanced at Arnold. 'Where exactly is the area you're concerned about?'

Arnold pointed towards the far corner of the building. 'There ... where the back lane runs towards the woods beyond.'

She nodded. 'I see ... Then I fear we might have a certain problem, Mr Landon. The work we are carrying on is internal, and some distance removed from the area you point to. But that area abuts on to the private abode of David Gilmagesh. I'm afraid we cannot allow access to that part of the building –'

'I'm not certain we would seek access,' Arnold explained. 'We would be working outside the main walls.'

'Even so ...' Sister Simone pursed her lips. 'We will have to consult on the matter. In fact ...' She paused, staring. Arnold glanced to the point she was observing. He saw that there was a Land Rover parked at the edge of the woods, and someone was standing on the drovers' track. He appeared to be observing Deerbolt Hall, and there was a brief flash of reflected sunlight from the binoculars he held to his eyes. Sister Simone turned away; her glance met Arnold's and she smiled a little grimly. 'That would be your friend Colonel McArdle,' she said.

Portia Tyrrel watched the distant figure for a moment. 'What's he doing there?'

'Trespassing,' Sister Simone replied dismissively. 'That land belongs to us. But for some reason he seems very interested in what we are doing here at Oclixtan. He visits regularly ... It is of little consequence to us: a minor irritation we can deal with adequately enough. Perhaps you'd like to follow me ...'

She led the way back down the narrow stairs and they followed her as she walked once again across the courtyard to the north-east corner of the building, through a fine entrance porch and into a broad corridor. A sturdy oak door barred the way: she opened it and they entered a wide room, the far end of which had been blocked by scaffolding and boards. The window was in the process of being bricked up, while above their heads an opening had been made in the wooden roof. The medieval timbers had been exposed and the heavy stone slabs removed from the outside while what seemed to be a large sheet of green

83

plastic covering had been stretched across the aperture. There were no workmen present but there were all the signs of recent activity, scattered rubble, tools, the paraphernalia of a building site. Beyond the walls, Arnold guessed, would lie the area that his department was interested in investigating.

'What exactly are you doing here?' Arnold asked.

'We are building a place of worship, appropriate to our needs. It is necessary that our meditations should take place in a room that allows our spirits to soar free. Below the roof there we shall have our route to the heavens – flight will be possible, the opportunities enjoyed by David himself will become available to all of us under his influence, and we shall travel among the stars ...' She stopped speaking and a silence descended upon them. Arnold felt his skin crawl, unaccountably: something stirred in his mind as he looked about him, the thought of flight among the stars bringing back faint memories of another time, another place ...

'I don't understand –'

'It will be a great window,' Sister Simone intoned. 'It will not affect the external appearance of the building so there need be no difficulties ... A great enclosed window, shielded by screens which at night will be drawn back, so that we can observe, feel, think and experience what David himself experiences. He will lead us into the cosmos; conduct us on our soul voyage, and bring us face to face with the true realities ...'

Her voice died away. She was staring at Arnold but it was as though she did not really see him. Then gradually the film cleared from her eyes. She smiled. 'So there is no need for you to be concerned with us. We are a closed order. We do nothing to offend others. We will not disturb your own researches. And you will not disturb ours.'

She turned to leave and Portia Tyrrel said, 'This leader of yours ... David Gilmagesh. Would we be able to see him?'

'There is no need. It is not possible.'

'He's not here at the moment?' Portia persisted.

'He is always here, in one form or another,' Sister Simone said dreamily.

'How do you mean?'

The hawkish features seemed irradiated; she stopped, looked

84

back, raised her glance to the half-finished window to the skies. 'We learn that the spirit of a person may be regarded as the essential existing force of that person. Without a spirit a person may occupy space and have weight, but would have no meaning and no real existence. But when a person is invested with the *inua* – what men call a soul – it is a part of nature of which we are aware. And David's *inua* is unique – it allows him to pass freely between the two worlds, throughout the cosmos, to journey in the spirit realm. We say to him *Takujumaqama – I come to you because I desire to see.* He is here and he is everywhere: he knows the music of the stars and the rhythms of the earth; he can ride to the moon in his separate realities; he is blind and yet a seer –'

'He's *blind*?' Portia asked in surprise.

The woman stared at her in surprise. There was a short pause. 'Sister Simone is speaking figuratively,' Arnold explained. 'But it's a pity we cannot meet Mr Gilmagesh . . .'

Sister Simone had stopped suddenly. Her head was cocked on one side, as though she were listening to something and then, after a short pause, she led the way out of the room, back into the corridor. When they emerged into the sunlight of the courtyard she raised a hand to shade her eyes.

Across the courtyard Arnold thought he saw a man, standing at the top of the steps to the main entrance. The glimpse was momentary; Arnold blinked in the sunlight and there was no one there. For a moment he thought it might have been merely a trick of the light, and that his eyesight had deceived him. Then Sister Simone sighed, and turned to look at him.

'He is here,' she said. 'He will see you now.'

2

The room was narrow, and dimly lit with candle-shaped lights set into the walls. The windows had been covered with heavy swagged curtains, and the walls also were shrouded in the same deep red materials that they had seen elsewhere. A heavy musk seemed to fill the air, the hint of a sleep-inducing incense; long forms were ranged along the walls, covered in silk, shot with red, piled with heavy cushions, and at the far end of the room was a raised dais on which was placed an altar-shaped table, swathed in heavy damask and similarly lined with deep cushions. There was an impression of sensuality in the room, a breathless feeling of drugged excitement, a slow, almost sexual tension that made the flesh tingle.

The man who stood in front of the dais could be seen only dimly in the faint light. He was perhaps five feet ten, Arnold guessed, slimly built, with a shock of blond hair. He was dressed in a loose flowing robe of deep red and blue, with the image of an animal wrought in gold along its length. It was difficult to ascertain his age, but Arnold guessed he was perhaps in his early forties. His face was thin; as he came forward to meet them a shaft of light seemed to illuminate his features and Arnold became aware of the intensity of his gaze, the sharp blue ice of his eyes. He stared at Arnold for a few moments, without speaking, and then he turned his gaze upon Portia.

'You are Portia Tyrrel. You are welcome. As are you, Mr Landon.'

Arnold felt Portia tense beside him; he knew she would be wondering how the man could know her name. It wasn't difficult to guess, Arnold concluded: one of the other acolytes could have brought him the message.

'I am David Gilmagesh.'

The voice was deep, confident and resonant, with a transatlantic accent. It was a practised voice, the tones honed to produce a definite effect. As though the thought was suddenly communicated, the ice-blue eyes swept in Arnold's direction. Gilmagesh smiled. 'You are satisfied with your visit. You are certain we are breaking no ... regulations?'

'Sister Simone has been kind enough to show us what is happening. It's a little early to say whether our plans at the Department of Museums and Antiquities might be disrupted. I'll need to take another look at the survey we had prepared back in Morpeth. We merely wanted to try to discover, today, whether our proposed investigations might be hampered —'

'And you are satisfied,' Gilmagesh interrupted imperiously,

giving Arnold no time to further qualify his remarks. 'But *you* are not,' he added, turning to Portia Tyrrel.

Her chin came up with a certain defiance. 'I'm sorry –'

'Your interest differs from that of Mr Landon. You are ... intrigued. You have questions of us here at Oclixtan.'

There was a short silence. Then Portia said, 'I am ... interested, yes. About what this is all about. Colonel McArdle –'

'Ah, yes, the colonel, the man who sees himself as our Nemesis ...'

'– Colonel McArdle suggested that this cult of yours might be dangerous in some way.'

'Dangerous?' Gilmagesh twitched his robe about him. 'In what way dangerous? We are a small group. We desire only to be left alone. Our search is for the inner soul: our road is flight through the cosmos. We have thrown aside the temptations and cares of the world and our community is as one. I am on a journey that reaches far beyond here – and I am followed, at a distance, by those who wish to follow, and who wish to experience what I have experienced.'

'So what is it you believe in?' Portia asked.

Gilmagesh smiled. He stepped back, away from them until his face was veiled in shadow again. It was Sister Simone who spoke, in a curiously sing-song tone, almost as though she was reciting some mantra. 'We believe in Oclixtan. We believe in the *nagual* from whose spirit David Gilmagesh sprang. We believe that his way is our way; that we should touch the world only sparingly; that we shall one day attain an increased level of awareness which will allow us to perform indescribable feats of perception and unequalled states of physical prowess and well-being. We shall master the art of dreaming. We shall travel the cosmos. We shall touch the energy of the heavens. Our ends are self-knowledge. And we shall never die.'

Her words seem to echo in the heaviness of the atmosphere. There was a short silence. Then Gilmagesh spoke again, almost dreamily. 'There is no death, in the ordinary sense. There is only transmutation: we are all the bearers of powers which must remain in the world of the living and I have received those powers and will hand them on to a successor. I am a protector spirit and I move through the landscape. I select my successors and I spread the Word. I cross the bleak lifeless steppes and I ascend the mountains of light; I descend through the jaws of the earth and I swim in the underground seas. The abyss is about me but I soar above it. I am Gilmagesh.'

He paused and the silence was heavy. There was a strange charged atmosphere about them suddenly, and the heavy, cloying scent in the air seemed to affect Arnold's senses. His mind side-slipped, he thought of space and time and whirling star shapes; a gulf seemed to open at his feet momentarily and there was the sound of music in his ears, the chanting of distant voices, the sense of electrical power leaping across the gaps in the universe. Then it faded as quickly as it seemed to have come, and he felt slightly dizzy. His eyes focused again. He felt cold.

In the dimness of the room, after what seemed an interminable time, the deep, resonant voice came again, almost in a whisper.

'I am Gilmagesh. I am Shaman.'

The sound fluttered about them, skittering under the roof, the soft whirring of a bird trying to escape from the room. Behind them Arnold heard a creaking sound. He and Portia both turned, involuntarily. The door behind them had opened, and a woman stood framed in the entrance. She was small, slight, dressed in the cowled grey cloak and red sash that seemed to be the uniform of the sisters.

'It is time to leave,' Sister Simone said quietly.

Arnold looked back. David Gilmagesh was no longer in the room.

They made their way back across the courtyard, accompanied by Sister Simone and the woman who had stood in the doorway. She kept her head down, but there was one brief glance from her towards Arnold that made him think she was about to say something. Perhaps the presence of Sister Simone suppressed the impulse. At the steps to the main entrance Sister Simone stopped.

'Sister Percepta will close the main gate after you leave. There will be no other visitors today.'

The silent woman called Percepta preceded them across to the car and stood with head bowed as they got in and Arnold started the engine. He drove towards the gate and slowed: through the rear mirror he could see that Sister Percepta had raised her head and was staring at them and he wondered again whether she had something she wanted to say. Then the cowled head was lowered once more, and when he looked back, driving down through the tree-lined carriageway, Arnold saw the gates closing behind them.

'So,' Portia Tyrrel breathed, 'what did you make of all that?'

'How do you mean?'

'Well, the whole thing! The controlled set-up . . . Sister Simone and Gilmagesh . . . the peculiar, sensual atmosphere . . . and didn't you feel anything a few minutes ago? Weren't you . . . affected in some way?'

Arnold was reluctant to discuss it. He glanced at Portia: her face was pale, her almond eyes troubled. 'I think we were overcome for a moment, by the atmosphere. It wasn't an accident. It would have been laid on for our benefit.'

She hardly seemed to hear him. Her brow was knitted in thought. 'How did he know our names, before we gave them?'

Arnold smiled cynically. 'Karen Stannard had arranged the visit. She probably told them who was coming. Or one of the acolytes – maybe the new one, Sister Percepta – had gone in to tell him ahead of our arrival in that peculiar reception room of his. If it was a reception room.'

'I don't know. To me it was more like a place where the sisters would congregate to worship at the feet of their leader. Or to do something even more sinister, in a brainwashed state. And after that . . . experience . . . Where did he go to suddenly? That shook me a bit . . .'

Arnold grimaced. It all smacked of charlatanism to him. The swift shaft of light that had illuminated the features of Gilmagesh; the drugged, heavy-scented air; the sudden impressions that had been forced into their minds; the unexplained disappearance when their attention was drawn elsewhere. It had been suggested to them that the man was a *nagual*, a shape-shifter, an embodiment of the spirits, a man who could be in two places at once. Again, a shadow crossed his mind, a recollection, too light and swift to be recaptured.

They drove in silence for a while, each busy with private thoughts. At last Portia sighed, seeming to discard her troubled imaginings, pulling herself together.

'What about the building work?' Portia asked. 'I suppose it's some kind of chapel they're constructing.'

Arnold shrugged. 'To that extent, we can't interfere. Internal works – even the changes to the roof – aren't something we can complain about, although I think the Planning Department ought to take another look at the whole thing. Maybe McArdle was right. Maybe they have been fooled in Planning. But what should concern *us* is the fact that we might be denied access for our own survey if we get too close to that part of Deerbolt – or should I say Oclixtan – that is designated for Gilmagesh's private use. Our studies may well bring us close to the walls . . .'

'I wonder what his real name is? I mean . . . *Gilmagesh*!'

Arnold smiled as he drove out of the avenue of trees and into the road beyond. 'I suppose it's a harmless enough subterfuge, to fool the impressionable.'

'Sister Simone is clearly impressionable.'

'Or clever,' Arnold submitted. 'It's obvious she's closely involved with Gilmagesh in the operation of the order. She'll be his main supporter, maybe his control mechanism. They have some way of communicating, no doubt, which is not immediately apparent . . . I mean, the decision to bring us to him, his disappearance when Sister Percepta suddenly arrived to escort us from the premises, the effect of the room itself . . . it's all set up, you know what I mean?'

'What I wonder about is how the whole thing is financed.' Portia shook her head doubtfully. 'Sister Simone avoided answering me, but Deerbolt Hall itself would have cost a packet, and then there's the development work that's going on. There are only twelve women there.'

'There might be a wider group subscribing to Oclixtan, beyond the group at the Hall itself.'

'Have you ever heard of them before?' Portia asked.

Arnold laughed. 'Oclixtan? I'm not exactly into cults of that kind. They're numerous enough, because there are more than enough gullible people out there, seeking some kind of explanation for their existence, some relief from their anxieties. And Gilmagesh is typical enough – a leader who has a certain presence, charisma, style, and a collection of myths, mumbo-jumbo and other claptrap designed to affect the senses, both verbally and physically . . .'

'So you didn't go along with the description of their beliefs,' she said mischievously.

'Hardly! It's all a mish-mash, a confusion, a drawing together of ideas and perceptions from other ancient beliefs. That talk of *inua*, for instance, it's from the Inuit superstition; a *nagual* has been described as the heir to the lineage of a Yaqui medicine man, a line of mystics stretching back to the Toltecs in pre-Hispanic Mexico; the reference to *Takujumaqama*, that's drawn from the Siberian belief that shamanic power is often expressed in terms of special sight.' He glanced at Portia. 'In that belief the eyes of the Siberian shaman were gouged out by spirit-blacksmiths and replaced by others which were adapted to see other realities. I doubt whether our friend Gilmagesh would go that far.'

'So you think he's a conman,' Portia said flatly.

Arnold considered the matter for a while in silence. Then he said, 'I think he's made a fairly extensive study of anthropological texts that have been published since the sixties. I think he's drawn from those studies a conglomeration of ideas and perceptions that he's moulded into a belief. I've no doubt that he's drawn around him a group of impressionable people whom he takes on a sort of psychedelic magical mystery tour – in which, quite possibly, some kind of drugs are used –'

'There was certainly some kind of heady scent pervading both those rooms we went into.'

'– and those robes he wore, the gold decoration . . . could you make out what it was?'

'I'm not sure . . .' she replied doubtfully.

'It was a stylised figure, a snarling jaguar,' Arnold informed her. 'And *that* comes from the Amazonian belief that there is a close identification between the animal itself, and the shaman. As I said, this man has pulled together a whole range, a hotch-potch of superstitions.'

91

Portia Tyrrel grunted. 'Well, it all reminded me of something else entirely.'

'And what's that?'

'The Agapemone,' she replied, hunching down in her seat.

3

The conference had been called in the west wing of the head-quarters at Ponteland. The buildings had previously been used as a teacher training college: its demise had meant that the police force had been able to acquire premises set in pleasant surroundings. The conference room had originally been one in which college governors had met. Now the Chief Constable presided at the head of a long, gleaming mahogany table.

When Culpeper entered he saw that Farnsby was already there, along with two strangers. The Chief Constable made the introductions. 'This is Inspector O'Connor, up from York. It was to support O'Connor that we seconded Farnsby a few weeks ago.'

Culpeper nodded and shook hands with the tall, saturnine-featured man in the dark grey suit. Sharp, he decided.

'And this is Inspector Garcia. Seconded to the same investigation, from Interpol.'

Culpeper's eyes widened. Things must be serious if Interpol had actually sent someone across. He liked the look of the man, though: easy manner, smiling eyes. His appearance could cover an inherent toughness, nevertheless.

'Well,' the Chief Constable said heavily once introductions were over, 'while this is not normally the kind of business I would interfere in, I thought that in view of the gravity of some of the suggestions emanating from the task group –' he inclined his head towards the three men facing Culpeper across the table – 'I'd better sit in on the discussion.'

'What are we here to talk about, sir?' Culpeper queried. He had enough already on his desk not to want to be drawn into matters that Farnsby had been delegated to attend to.

The Chief Constable sniffed. He was well used to Culpeper kicking against the traces. But it would not be too long now before the man would be put out to pasture. 'We're here to talk about the task force's conclusions, drawn from their enquiries, and how those conclusions might have an impact on our own responsibilities here in Northumberland. Farnsby?'

Inspector Farnsby caught Culpeper's glance but showed no discomfort. He had the Chief Constable to back him. 'As you know, sir, I've been seconded to work with Inspector O'Connor and Inspector Garcia on an investigation concerning a headless male corpse pulled out of the sea off Whitby. We have now been able to identify the man – as far as it's possible – as one Timothy Brazil. Interpol have been able to demonstrate that Brazil was active in the drug trade, and they were on the point of hauling him in, since it seems he had got into some kind of trouble with his criminal colleagues, when he set off on his yacht the *Dawn Princess*. His body turned up off Whitby: a search is still continuing for the yacht but it is suspected that it may have been scuttled . . .'

Culpeper stifled a yawn. He'd been up late last night, poring over some files. His wife had not been pleased, but then, he was well used to her displeasure. They had more or less agreed to differ on so many issues, and she had always been an outspoken Durham lass . . . He wondered briefly how they would get on in his retirement . . .

'Brazil had boarded the yacht with two other men. We're pretty sure now that one of them was an American called Jordan. It's a matter of some curiosity that Jordan was traced as having returned to Barcelona *after* the yacht sailed, and took a flight to Newcastle. Since then, we've not managed to lay a handle on him.'

Culpeper looked at the Chief Constable in supplication. 'I'm sorry, sir, but have I been called into this conference to assist in finding this man Jordan in Newcastle? If so, I really have to say that I'm up to my ears already, and Farnsby –'

'Mr Culpeper,' the Chief Constable warned, a dangerous rumble in his tone, 'I think you'd better wait for a moment. You've always been inclined to remind us that your background is different from Inspector Farnsby's. You are the man who came up the traditional route, via the beat; you are the man who knows Tyneside and Tynesiders. So give us the benefit of your . . . patience.'

Culpeper glowered. He looked at Farnsby, and at the two men seated beside him. 'It just seems to me that there's enough people on this already. A task force using three men of inspector rank –'

'Culpeper –'

Farnsby cut in on the Chief Constable, unwilling to get involved in an argument that could end only in one way. 'It's just that we need some contact names, sir,' he said to Culpeper. 'The fact of the matter is, we've lost sight of Jordan, but we know that he arrived. And we also now know that there are rumours on Tyneside of a new operation along the river. The Newcastle force is co-operating with us, as is that of Cleveland through Inspector O'Connor, but this operation also extends into Shields, and –'

'Operation?'

'Drugs,' Inspector Garcia said quietly, his dark eyes fixed on Culpeper.

There was a short silence. At last, Culpeper asked, 'What do you mean by contacts?'

Eagerly, Farnsby said, 'Inspector O'Connor has his own network stretching into Middlesbrough and Teesport generally. He's been informed that new supplies are coming in, but they seem to be concentrated on shipments from the Tyne. Inspector Garcia feels it may well be this man Jordan who is setting up the new supply route: Interpol has been able to confirm the closing down of some activities previously undertaken by the dead man, Timothy Brazil. In other words, there's the suspicion that there's been a transference of activity from Barcelona, where things were being run through Brazil, to Newcastle. Where a new system has been set up by Jordan.'

'I'm still not quite clear . . .'

O'Connor leaned forward, one elbow on the table. 'We're proceeding on the hypothesis that Timothy Brazil fell out with his suppliers in Spain. We think maybe they discovered he had sticky fingers, he tried to get away from his colleagues, but was taken on board his own yacht by the American operators in the syndicate. He was killed, dumped overboard, and while one man took the yacht and either scuttled it or hid it somewhere along the coast, the other – Charlie Jordan – came back to Barcelona, either to clean things up or to meet the syndicate organisers, before making his way to Newcastle. There's even the thought that he might be involved as the main supplier in the States.'

'But why Tyneside?' Culpeper asked. 'If Jordan was replacing this villain Brazil, why didn't he simply take up the reins in Barcelona? Why go to the trouble of setting up an entirely new operation up here in the north?'

There was a short silence. At last, Garcia shrugged. 'We don't know. But the facts – as far as we've been able to ascertain them – are as we've given you.'

'It's all pretty thin. If this is all you've been able to come up with, when three of you are working on the case –'

'That's why we'd like your assistance,' O'Connor interrupted grimly. 'I'm told you're an old-fashioned copper, with old-fashioned contacts. My father was the same kind. And he could get results in ways I never could.'

Culpeper was pleased, in spite of himself. He held O'Connor's glance, wary that the man might be flannelling him, but mollified, nevertheless. 'You want me to dig up my contacts, see if there are any snouts along the river who can get some information . . .'

'That's it precisely,' O'Connor nodded.

'And I don't think it should involve you too much, sir,' Farnsby interrupted. 'If you can give us some names, we'd be able to . . .'

He became aware of the frostiness in Culpeper's eyes. 'That would be a mistake, bonny lad. Things don't work like that on the street. It's years since I pounded the beat on Tyneside, but the West End hasn't forgotten me up here, and I'm still well enough remembered in Shields. But they don't know *you*, or your task force . . . and this is not the kind of thing you can crack by going around with a letter of recommendation in your hand. Of course it's going to take time, and there's no other way of doing it than by doing it myself – when I'm already up to my bloody ears in work!'

There was an uncomfortable silence. It was broken finally by the Chief Constable. With an air of cool indifference, he asked, 'Just what *are* your priorities at the moment, Culpeper?'

'If you mean my caseload, sir, I should remind you that you yourself dictated some of them. Not least the matter of Colin Ledbury.'

The Chief Constable wrinkled his nose. 'Ledbury. Ah . . . yes. He's been trying to discover what's happened to his sister. Have you . . . er . . . have you found out anything yet?'

'About just where she's got to, no,' Culpeper replied. He could not resist the note of triumph when he went on, 'but about your young friend Ledbury, well, that's another matter.'

The Chief Constable glared. He glanced at the others in the room. 'Mr Culpeper is using language loosely, of course. Colin Ledbury is no friend . . . not even an acquaintance of mine. But he is a member of a respected family in the area, and we don't want any further scandals –'

'Ah, well, that's just it, sir,' Culpeper interrupted cheerfully. 'I've been making enquiries, as you asked. Some local . . . some down in London. My own little task force, you might say, sir. And I find that our Mr Ledbury is in a bit of financial trouble.' He beamed at Inspector Garcia. 'They have trouble with drugs down in London too, you know.'

'Get on with it, Culpeper,' the Chief Constable snapped in an irritated tone.

'It seems that our young friend Colin Ledbury hasn't entirely escaped the consequences of his rather wild teenage years,' Culpeper explained. 'For your information, gentlemen, he's been a bit of a scallywag and the despair of his family for some years. Scion of a noble family he might be –'

'Culpeper . . .' the Chief Constable warned.

'– but he's been a bit of a tearaway, on the edge of the drug scene, bit of assault here, battery there, short term inside . . . all that sort of stuff. Bad company, of course. But he always felt that things would turn out well in the end with an ailing father, and landed estates waiting for him in Northumberland. The Ridgeway estates, in fact, prime land and extensive holdings. And as the only son . . .'

Culpeper grinned at the Chief Constable. 'I'm not certain, sir, whether it involved any of your . . . ah . . . acquaintances in the county, but there's certainly a rumour about some kind of syndicate set up to profit from the Ridgeway landholdings. It seems a group got together to set up some building development . . . I've not got the actual details yet, because it seems no plans have been filed in the Planning Department at Morpeth, but the little birds tell me that Colin Ledbury is part of the whole business. He seems to have committed himself to a bit of legitimate action at last . . . though he does need money to buy into the syndicate, and there's also the question of the land, of course . . .'

The Chief Constable was irritated, but interested also. 'Just what are you getting at, Culpeper?'

Culpeper sighed dramatically. 'Well, it's all a bit sad, really. Young Ledbury, with a misspent youth behind him, gets pulled into a consortium deal . . . I'm a bit vague on personnel, but I gather it contains some pretty well-known people in the county. The Ridgeway estate is central to the plan, and Ledbury's only too keen to get involved but he's still down in London, and his father's sort of banned him from the ancestral home, so he gets hold of one of his acquaintances to keep an eye on things. A man called Carter. Bit of a thug, actually, but maybe Ledbury doesn't know too many of the other kind in the north. Anyway, it was all looking to be good when the old man finally turned up his toes and died. Ledbury immediately set about sacking the staff, and put Carter in as estate manager, while he told the consortium they could start putting things together at last. Unfortunately . . .'

He paused triumphantly, aware that he held the interest of the men facing him. 'Unfortunately, the old man had cut him out of the will. He doesn't get title to the lands. They go to his sister – who, like young Colin, has been living well away from the family mansion. Not a close group at all, father, son and daughter . . . But with a choice between them, well, the old man made his decision and it's she who's copped it all. She comes back for the reading of the will, installs herself in the old homestead, and our Colin is more than a little . . . pissed off, shall we say? Especially when, as I'm reliably informed, she's not very interested in this consortium deal at all. And then he prances up to us here, a few months later, and announces his sister has disappeared, and what are we going to do about it?'

The Chief Constable leaned forward grimly. 'Culpeper, are you sure about this?'

'About his coming here to ask for our assistance?' Culpeper teased.

'No, dammit,' the Chief Constable snapped, empurpling. 'About this consortium business, and Ledbury being involved –'

'You mean they hadn't told you, sir?' Culpeper asked innocently.

There was a short silence. The Chief Constable stared at Culpeper, and slowly began to drum his fingers on the table in front of him. He seemed lost in thought, but the thoughts were clearly not pleasant. He was not enjoying being baited by the detective chief inspector, but there were also signs of anger at the implication that he had been kept in the dark about certain facts, by friends of his in the county set.

'Of course,' Culpeper suggested, 'I could pull back on this Ledbury business. I mean, it's not all that important, is it? There's no evidence that I've been able to turn up that Miss Grace Ledbury – Colin's sister – has been subjected to any suspicious interference. I mean, she's of full age, she can wander where she wants to, and she's got plenty of money to do what she wants. Unless, of course, there's the thought that maybe Colin Ledbury's playing a deep game. Maybe he's reported her disappearance in order to cover his tracks. Maybe he himself has had something to do with her disappearance; maybe he's got some idea of how he can get his hands on the money that's been denied him, by spiriting away his sister. Who knows? I mean, I haven't been able to find out where she's gone, but we could extend our enquiries, if you really believe he's involved in some skulduggery ...' Culpeper looked around the room at the silent men facing him and smiled. 'As I said before, I'd just like to know what my priorities should be ...'

The Chief Constable seemed to be struggling with himself, not certain what to say. His brows were drawn together, and he seemed on the verge of losing his temper. He was saved by a nervous tap on the door. It opened: a uniformed sergeant stuck his head into the room. The Chief Constable glared at him. 'Yes?'

'Phone call, sir.'

'Important?'

The sergeant grimaced. 'They say . . .'

'All right, I'll take it.' It was one way of recovering his equilibrium. He stood up and walked across to the table at the side of the room and lifted up the extension phone. He listened for a few minutes, without expression. At last he put the phone down, and returned to his seat at the conference table. He sat there silently, looking around at the expectant faces. He clucked his tongue angrily. 'There's been another development, gentlemen.'

They waited. The Chief Constable looked at Culpeper. 'You've been complaining about priorities. Well, I'll help you. It looks as though the task force will have to wait: do what you can to assist them, with names of any snouts along the river that you think can help. As for the Ledbury business . . . let it lie. I have some questions I want to pursue on that one myself . . . But for now, *you* have a new priority. You'd better get up to Riggs Manor, immediately.'

'I drop the Ledbury enquiry? What's happened, sir?'

'I'm afraid, gentlemen,' the Chief Constable said heavily, glancing at the task force, 'in the matter of priorities, if we have a possible murder on our own patch, it will have to take precedence over a missing young woman who may have her own perfectly valid reasons for walking away from her brother, and the possible emergence of a new drugs baron on Tyneside – which is, after all, more properly the province of the Newcastle police . . .'

He stared at Culpeper, almost accusingly. 'It seems that a Colonel McArdle has seen fit to jump from the bell tower in his own home. But . . . there is also the thought that he might have been . . . assisted in his . . . ah . . . flight . . .'

PART FOUR

1

Culpeper scowled. He did not like Inspector Farnsby, but he had to admit he was a good copper and nobody's fool. He could have done with Farnsby in looking around Riggs Manor: the man had a good eye. And Culpeper did not feel he could trust the raw sergeant assigned to help him on the McArdle investigation: inexperience could mean lost evidence or mistaken assumptions.

At least there weren't very many people to interview. Colonel McArdle had employed only part-time staff and none of them had been on the premises when he had fallen to his death.

Bad-temperedly, Culpeper ascended the narrow staircase to the bell tower and prowled about the crenellated platform. It was a sunny day, and the clear skies meant he could enjoy splendid views, but he was not in the mood to take pleasure in the rolling hills and green woodland. He had almost enjoyed baiting the Chief Constable the previous day, but in the end he had gained little by it: he had not managed to obtain the services of Inspector Farnsby and he had been saddled with another problem on his caseload. And there was nothing to be seen up here: the woman who came in to do the cooking had found the colonel in the courtyard and had run yelling to the phone. Culpeper peered over the parapet and looked down: it was quite a fall and it had made quite a mess of Colonel McArdle's skull. The dark stain of blood was still visible on the paving stones below. But apart from that, there was no sign of anything odd up here on the platform.

He made his way back down the stairs and into the main house. Detective Sergeant Tashent was in the study: a stocky, black-haired man with dark skin and a constant stubble shadow. Culpeper reckoned he had Russian blood. He wondered what the hell had brought him to the north-east. The Baltic Exchange maybe, two generations ago. He had a Geordie accent, at least. Certainly not Russian.

Culpeper dropped into the leather-covered easy chair in front of the desk and eyed the sergeant. 'Well, what've we got, then?'

Tashent unfolded his notebook and studied it intently for a few moments. 'The possibility of suicide is still not entirely ruled out, sir, but the people we've interviewed suggest that it's unlikely – in their view the colonel was an active, community-minded man who had showed no signs of depression. Indeed, he was quite busy, with his fingers in a number of pies, and everyone expresses surprise and shock at his demise.'

Surprise, shock . . . and demise. He *had* to be Russian, with such precise English. Culpeper eyed the sergeant sourly. He'd had enough of that sort of chatter from Farnsby over the years. And he didn't believe Tashent spoke like that at home in Longbenton. 'So run over the interviews again.'

Tashent nodded. 'It was the part-time cook who found him. The colonel was already dead . . . probably from the night before because there'd been a light rain and his clothes were wet. She reckons the front door was unlocked, and that was unusual: he was a security-conscious man. Also, there were signs that some-one had been at the manor visiting the colonel –'

'A visitor for dinner?'

'No, that was never done. If McArdle had company, he arranged for outside caterers. On this occasion, it seems, some-one came for drinks only.'

Outside caterers. Maybe he should have tried that years ago, Culpeper thought, recalling numerous dyspeptic occasions. 'Drinks, hey? Glasses with Forensic?'

Tashent nodded. 'Not much point, though. The glasses had been washed clean. The visitor must have been a tidy person.'

'Or a careful one,' Culpeper growled.

Tashent consulted his notes again. 'I've spoken to the gar-deners, and the cleaners, and they have nothing significant to add. They saw McArdle in the morning and he seemed in good spirits – in fact, he seemed pleased as much as anything. He was out during the afternoon, took his Land Rover . . .'

'Do we know where he went?'

Tashent shrugged. 'We've not been able to trace his move-ments, sir. Except we know he was back at Riggs Manor by about five thirty, because one of the gardeners saw him arrive, as he himself was leaving. The colonel must have received his company some time after that.'

'Woman?'

Tashent shook his head. 'No way of knowing. But the colonel – a widower – is reputed to have had an eye for the ladies.'

Culpeper sighed. His wife had warned him many years ago, that way lay disaster. 'So what exactly made you think this was murder, rather than suicide? It *was* you who rang in, wasn't it?'

Tashent was uncomfortable, Culpeper could tell. He wriggled a little, in that Russian way of his. 'Well, I couldn't be sure, sir. I was called out, and those I spoke to said they didn't think he was the suicide type, and I wasn't really sure of the procedures, so I thought it best to play safe. The Forensic people were here and . . .' His voice tailed off uncertainly.

Culpeper shook his head. This would have been Tashent's first violent death. He could have done with Farnsby. He was from Durham, and used to mayhem. Culpeper gestured around the study. 'Have you had a good look around here?'

'No, sir, I was about to do so when you arrived, so I thought . . .'

Culpeper swung around in the leather chair. He inspected the desk. It was neat and tidy, as one would expect of an ex-military man. Everything seemed to have been arranged with parade ground precision: writing pad, pens, paperweights, notebook, calculator. There was a computer placed squarely on a side table. Culpeper eyed it sourly: he had never quite taken to the communications revolution. 'I suppose you're familiar with those things?'

Tashent nodded. 'I have some skills –'

'Open it up, then, and check what files he's got, and what's on them.'

Methodically, he himself began to check through the drawers of the leather-topped desk: bank account statements, scissors, stamps, odd keys, an old camera, miscellaneous papers . . . and a diary. Eagerly he opened it, turned it to the day on which McArdle had died. There were no entries for that day, so it

105

seemed McArdle had either invited his guest relatively late in the day, or the visitor had arrived unexpectedly.

'There are about thirty current files here, sir,' Tashent said, peering at the blue screen in front of him. 'He was a methodical man, the colonel. Kept everything precise and tidy, like. There's a file on Riggs Manor itself, a few that look like military notes, something to do with the Ridgeway estate –'

'Hold on, hold on,' Culpeper said. 'The Ridgeway estate? What's that all about?'

Tashent was silent for a few moments as he scanned the details of the file on the screen in front of him. 'Some sort of quarrel, it seems, sir. Boundary difficulties, or something.'

'All right. There's a printer attached? Better print out that file . . . and trawl through the rest of them for possible leads. Better print everything out, in fact, so we can read the stuff at our leisure. Though that's a laugh. Leisure . . .'

He turned his attention back to the diary in his hands. He flicked back through the pages: they contained notes of various activities McArdle had been involved in, and various people with whom he had been in contact. He caught sight of a familiar name.

Landon.

Culpeper twisted his lip, tugged at it thoughtfully with finger and thumb. There was another name beside Landon. Tyrrel. It was followed by two exclamation marks. And it seemed that Landon and this Tyrrel person had had dinner with Colonel McArdle, after some kind of meeting at Warkworth . . . It was something Culpeper had better follow up. He wondered what had been meant by the exclamation marks.

Karen Stannard's grey-green eyes held a hint of calculation as she stared at Arnold and Portia Tyrrel. She was wearing a dark, sharply cut jacket over a white silk shirt, and her left hand had slipped inside the jacket, caressing the silk on her shoulder. 'So you think we shouldn't just leave them to get on with it up at Deerbolt Hall?'

Arnold dragged his attention away from the provocative, caressing hand and glanced at Portia. He shook his head. 'The set-up there is all a bit ... odd, but that really isn't the point. I suspect that the Planning Department did not in fact carry out as thorough an investigation of the building works proposed as maybe they should have done –'

'But that's not our business,' Karen Stannard interrupted evenly.

'Of course not. But as far as we're concerned, there is the danger we might find damage has occurred to the area we wish to excavate. I can't be sure, but my guess is that there'll be some intrusion to the site, and in any case if we don't undertake some work soon, I have the feeling David Gilmagesh might prevent us getting access. They're a somewhat exclusive cult, and they'll get more and more secretive as time goes on, I would guess.'

'What did *you* make of them, Portia?' Karen asked silkily. Her glance slid to her assistant, weighing up her appearance in the way only a woman could, and though her eyes seemed dark and thoughtful, there was a deep glint in them that made Arnold think of a predatory feline. He suddenly felt very much out of his depth, in the presence of some kind of inexplicable, unstated, sensual confrontation.

Portia's features were calm: she always seemed unaffected by Karen Stannard's moods. She was, Arnold thought, being particularly Asian.

'Like Arnold,' she said smoothly, 'I think they're somewhat ... kinky. It's a cult, of course, and a con, I'm fairly sure. Though the effects are good, I have to admit. As to the secrecy thing, I'm sure Arnold is right –'

'*Arnold* usually is,' Karen said mockingly, her glance slipping provocatively towards him.

'I'm sure that's so,' Portia replied demurely, ignoring the jibe. 'But I think the secrecy will get tighter, because the whole thing reminds me of the Agapemone.'

'You mentioned that earlier,' Arnold said. 'I didn't understand the reference.'

Portia raised a cool eyebrow. 'No? I'm sure Miss Stannard must have heard of it. The Agapemone was a sort of cult that appeared in the middle of the last century, in Victorian England. It caused quite a sensation at the time. It was run by a man called Prince; I can't remember what his claims were exactly, in religious terms, but the idea was that he ran this private worshipping thing down in Devon, at Charlinch, near Taunton. It involved all sorts of mumbo-jumbo, but he claimed to be divine, drew around him quite a group of impressionable people to whom he promised immortality, and they lived in a large house in its own grounds and did their own peculiar thing, religiously speaking. It was only when one or two of the families of people involved took the matter to court that it all leaked out.'

'What leaked out?'

Portia pursed her lips primly. 'The sexual practices. It seemed Prince persuaded his acolytes – who were mainly women – that immortality had a price. Their route to eternal life lay by offering themselves at the altar. Mr Prince took the part of the heavenly conduit, of course. The women gave up their virginity to him in a public religious ceremony, stretched out on the altar, and everyone applauded and praised God. Or Mr Prince, anyway. Each occasion was quite an event, it seemed – the women found it an uplifting experience.'

Arnold eyed her carefully. He could not be certain how serious she was.

'Oh, and another thing,' Portia added. 'There was an entry fee – apart from the surrendering of virginity, I mean. They had to make over to Prince all their worldly goods. And most of them were rather rich, as well as impressionable, ladies.'

There was a short silence. Like Arnold, Karen Stannard was a little taken aback, out of balance. 'The Agapemone . . .'

'It means "The Abode of Love".'

'And you think that up at Deerbolt Hall –'

'Oh, I've no idea if Gilmagesh is screwing the hell out of the twelve sisters of Oclixtan,' Portia Tyrrel said happily, 'but the order does consist merely of women, there is a sensuous feel about the place, silks, deep cushions, incense . . . You should go up there sometime, Miss Stannard. I'm sure you'd find it . . . affecting.'

Arnold hardly dared look at Karen. He was convinced she would be smouldering, but unable to pin down what she should be angry about. He looked at her: the green eyes were blazing but she kept control of herself. For the time being. Arnold began to wonder whether Portia Tyrrel would suffer for her daring. Or maybe the acting director of the Department of Museums and Antiquities had met her match at last, even if in a subordinate.

'I don't think a visit from me personally would serve any real purpose,' Kareh said cuttingly. She glanced at Arnold. 'But I think I'm inclined to take up your suggestion. It's going to be difficult to transfer the necessary funds, in an already tight budget, but I think you yourself had better make arrangements to begin the site survey we'd planned some time ago.' Her glance slipped back, thoughtfully, to Portia. 'However, I don't think *you* need to go back up there again, Portia. I wouldn't wish your continued exposure to such ... *erotic* influences, since they've clearly made such an *impression* on you. I do have a duty to protect my staff, after all, even from themselves ...'

Portia Tyrrel joined Arnold as he walked along the corridor back to his room. There was a subdued giggle in her voice. 'I reckon she'd just *love* to go up there and meet David Gilmagesh. Do you think she'd be a match for him?'

'More than a match,' Arnold replied. 'Believe me!'

They turned the corner in the corridor. The door to his office was open, and he could make out someone sitting in the chair in front of his desk. With Portia still beside him he entered the office. The man in the chair stood up, turning. He looked at Arnold, then his glance slid past to Portia Tyrrel. Unaccountably, he murmured, 'Exclamation marks!'

It was Detective Chief Inspector Culpeper.

'So what exactly was it that you discussed with Colonel McArdle when you had dinner with him?' Culpeper asked as he lounged in the chair in front of Arnold's desk.

Landon himself still seemed stunned at the news that McArdle had died in a fall from the bell tower at Riggs Manor. Portia Tyrrel on the other hand seemed to have taken it with more equanimity. Culpeper was interested in her: he could understand McArdle's comment in his diary. Culpeper had learned that

Colonel McArdle had had a certain reputation, as an admirer, if not a chaser of women, and he would have enjoyed meeting the delectable Miss Tyrrel. Culpeper wondered vaguely how Landon managed to maintain his work schedules, being in daily contact with such remarkably beautiful women as Karen Stannard and Portia Tyrrel. It must be a job in a million.

'I'd given a talk at the antiquarian society,' Landon said vaguely. 'He invited us back to dinner because he wanted to make certain complaints.'

'About what?' Culpeper asked sharply.

Landon glanced at Portia, as though for support. 'Well, in the first instance it seems he was having a running battle with the Ridgeway estate, over a matter of boundaries . . .'

Culpeper raised his eyebrows in surprise, and was silent for a little while. At last he murmured, 'Ah . . . yes. Tell me about that. Would it have been in connection with a projected building development?'

Surprise stained Landon's voice. 'That's right. You know about it? No application has been made to the Planning Department, but McArdle seemed convinced that there was some kind of development in the wind, and he was extremely angry about what he saw as an encroachment on his own land. It would have been a service road for the development, or something of the kind, it seems . . . but I'm not too clear what it was all about.'

'I see . . . And this argument he was having, it wouldn't have been with the owner – the *previous* owner of the estate?'

'I don't think so. He died, I believe, before the problem arose. No, as far as I could make out the argument was sort of by proxy.'

'How do you mean?' Culpeper asked.

'McArdle had clashed not with the present owner of the estate . . . it was with the estate manager. I don't think he ever even met the new owner.'

'And the estate manager was a man called Carter.'

'You know him?'

Culpeper nodded thoughtfully. 'Aye, I've come across Carter. A hard man . . .'

110

'McArdle seemed to think so.'

'So that was all you discussed with McArdle?'

Portia Tyrrel leaned forward. Her skin was flawless, her dark eyes bright and sincere as she fixed her gaze on Culpeper. 'There was also the matter of Deerbolt Hall. Oddly enough, we've just been talking about it with Miss Stannard.'

Culpeper did not regard himself as particularly susceptible to beautiful women. But there was something different about Portia Tyrrel. A man didn't come across too many women with an Asian cast of features in the north-east, and certainly not one so beautiful, poised and in control. And, he suspected, always with her own agenda. 'What about Deerbolt Hall?'

'It was the colonel's other preoccupation . . .'

Culpeper doubted that, observing the soft curve of her mouth, and recalling the exclamation marks in the man's diary.

'. . . He was very much . . . occupied with what was going on at Deerbolt.'

'And what *was* going on at Deerbolt?' Culpeper asked, fascinated in spite of himself.

She shrugged prettily. Her almond eyes slid towards her companion. 'Arnold and I were up there recently. There's a sort of cult moved in there. They call themselves . . . Oclixtan. And McArdle didn't like what they were about.'

'For what reason?'

'He suspected they were undertaking development work there for which they had not obtained planning permission. All very boring, really, but he was very keen that something should be done about it. He was chairman of a local antiquarian society and he tended to have rather strong views about such things . . . And he was certainly keeping an eye on them. I mean, the day Arnold and I were there, we saw him parked near the woods on the hill. He was using binoculars.' She made it sound a very sinister activity. Her voice died away and she watched Culpeper with innocent eyes. 'But I can't imagine that Oclixtan activities would cause him such anxiety and concern that he would throw himself from the bell tower. But . . . you didn't say, exactly, Chief Inspector. Did he jump . . . or was he *pushed*?'

Culpeper stared at her, almost mesmerised, and then he pulled

111

himself together. He took a deep breath. You may well ask, he thought to himself grimly.

When he made his way back to the Ponteland headquarters Culpeper was vaguely dissatisfied. He did not feel he had obtained anything really constructive from his brief talk with Landon and Portia Tyrrel. No questions had been resolved. On the other hand, there was the matter of the Ridgeway estate: Landon and Portia Tyrrel had confirmed what he himself had already heard, and what was actually on the file McArdle had kept on his computer. He was also interested in the involvement of Carter. The hard man had clearly been put in as estate manager to watch out for Colin Ledbury's interests, and that in itself was worth looking at.

But a good copper didn't get bogged down in one rut in an enquiry. Certainly, if there was a neighbour making a noise about boundaries when an important building development was possibly in the offing, Carter would have been a useful man to have around ... but was the matter serious enough to warrant even a suspicion that it might have been resolved by Carter throwing McArdle off the bell tower? After all, the scheme was in abeyance, because Colin Ledbury didn't own the land anyway.

As for the Deerbolt Hall thing, what was *that* all about? Could McArdle really have been all that excited about a cult knocking walls about in Deerbolt Hall? And could he really have made such a nuisance of himself up there that someone at Deerbolt would have wanted to get rid of him? It all seemed too thin.

Culpeper parked his car in the usual spot at Ponteland. He made his way up to his office, scowling at the pile of untouched files on his desk. It was time Farnsby got hauled back from his so-called task force with O'Connor and Garcia, and helped clear the backlog. He sat down behind his desk and was immediately irritated by a knock on the door.

'Yes? What is it?'

Detective Sergeant Tashent stuck his dark head around the door and grimaced apologetically. 'Sorry to disturb you, sir, but I called in at the forensic laboratories in Gosforth this afternoon.'

'Don't tell me they've already got something! They usually take weeks, and even then it's usually bloody inconclusive.'

Tashent bobbed his head uncertainly. 'I wouldn't know about that, sir. But they suggested I let you have this brief report – sort of initial findings. They think it might be of some importance. It's about something they found, during the autopsy.'

He handed the brief report to Culpeper. He read it, uncomprehendingly.

'Peyote? What the hell is that?'

Tashent shook his head. 'I'm not certain, sir. I had a chat with Dr Enders about it. He says that the brain produces a natural hormone, called noradrenaline, and the chemical structure of noradrenaline is very similar to that of peyote. The result is to induce euphoria, sometimes amnesia, and even an altered state of consciousness. It reduces the body's sensitivity to pain: the endorphins produced are similar to morphine and by attaching themselves to the receptors, or nerve cells . . .'

His voice died away, under Culpeper's glare. 'What the hell are you talking about, Tashent?'

'They found traces, sir. In McArdle's body.'

'Of what?'

'It's called peyote, sir . . .' He shrugged, unhappily.

Culpeper's incomprehension was complete.

2

Late afternoon clouds had built up threateningly above the Cheviots but bright patches of sunshine outlined the near hills as Arnold drove from Morpeth headquarters along the familiar road to Deerbolt Hall. He had taken the precaution, before leaving the office, of having a further discussion with Fred Orrell in the Planning Department to explain some of his concerns; Orrell had responded by showing him the inspector's report on the changes that had been identified with the Oclixtan group. Arnold noted with interest that there had been no contact with David Gilmagesh himself: it had been Sister Simone who showed the inspector around and explained the changes to him.

Arnold had rung ahead to Deerbolt Hall, and he was expected, so the great front gate was open and he was able to drive into the courtyard beyond, and park near the entrance steps. Sister Simone was standing there when he got out of his car.

'I hardly expected to be seeing you again so soon, Mr Landon.'

There was a certain severity about her mouth, and her eyes were watchful. Arnold gestured towards the far end of the courtyard. 'You were kind enough to show me what you were doing internally to the roof, but as you know, we'd served notice on the previous owners of Deerbolt that we wished to undertake some investigative excavations at the external rear walls. The funding is now likely to be available so we thought it would be a good idea to check the site again, and then ask you formally for reconfirmation –'

'So what is it you want now?' she interrupted him. 'Do you need to come inside, because it is somewhat inconvenient. The sisters will be at their devotions.'

Arnold shook his head. 'No, I don't need to come in. It might be useful if I could have another word with Mr Gilmagesh later, perhaps.'

'I'm afraid that won't be possible,' Sister Simone said bleakly. 'Our leader is away at the moment – he is speaking up at Wark, with a small group of persons who are desirous of supporting our search for the truth.'

'Ah. Well, as I said, I don't need to come inside. I just have to look at the area to the rear of the Hall.'

'In his absence,' Sister Simone continued, 'I am empowered to speak for the order.'

'Then I'll call to see you when my work is done,' Arnold said, and turned away.

He walked back through the main gateway and made his way around to the rear of Deerbolt Hall, scrambling across a low fence, and crossing a narrow bridge that he guessed would have seen service for at least two hundred years as part of the drovers' way. To his left, cresting the rise, was the strip of woodland where he had on his last visit to Deerbolt seen Colonel McArdle parked, watching the Hall, eager to protect the interests of his antiquarian society. Arnold suspected that without the energetic lead of the colonel, the antiquarian society he had talked to at Warkworth would probably now wither and die. Only the Antiquities and Museums Department would continue to have a further interest in what was going on at Deerbolt Hall.

He walked a short distance along the drovers' way. He had deliberately chosen to come here when the day was well advanced because the late afternoon sun would throw long shadows that would make it easier to see irregularities in the landscape: the kind of irregularities that could highlight the fact that man-made works had been constructed in the field outside the Hall. From half-way up the hill he had a good view of the rear of the big house, and could see its layout more clearly. He was looking straight down into the private area at the back designated for the use of David Gilmagesh himself, while to the left of that wing was the 'chapel' where the roof was being reconstructed to allow Gilmagesh and his followers to experience their travel into the cosmos. He smiled wryly. It all smacked very much of what Professor Schwartz had been talking about in the Mojave desert.

The thought troubled him; he felt guilty he hadn't spoken to Jane recently – and he had still given no answer to Schwartz's offer of a job at the university. It was a decision he would have to make soon.

He stayed where he was on the hill for half an hour or so, carefully checking the ground that lay between him and the Hall itself. The drovers' track was clearly enough visible: remains of a stone surface, worn, trodden, hard-packed earth greened over but still visible as an indentation across the field. There were some shadowed areas when the slanting sun picked out irregular shapes, possibly the location of medieval structures, and closer to the rear walls of the Hall the ground was raised in several places. From the survey undertaken a few years previously they had been designated as the possible sites of buildings, either used as rest houses or taverns by the drovers, or the remains of a medieval market, just outside the existing walls of the Hall.

Deerbolt Hall itself had had a rear entrance through which access would have been possible to travellers. It was just possible to make out the outline of stonework that had been used to close the access at some stage. It was close to the chapel area where work for the cult was being undertaken. It required closer investigation. Arnold stowed the folded survey map in his pocket and walked along the drovers' track towards the area he was interested in.

He kept his eyes down, following the track. He wondered just how old it really was. There was the possibility it could be Saxon, or even earlier: Romans and Vikings might have trodden this trail; it might have been neolithic in origin. Who was to tell now? Roadways of this kind were notoriously difficult to date. He stopped in the shadow of the walls of Deerbolt and he thought back to the way it must have been, the scene that must have been presented in the ancient days when lowing cattle had been driven along this stone track, to the pens that would have been available across to the left, while the drovers rested, and ate and drank and slept in wooden hovels, long since swept away.

And as he thought about those long dead days something prickled at the back of his neck. It was as though he felt their presence, those men who had passed this way. Their voices seemed to echo in the valley; there was a cold breath in his hair, the rustle of a breeze bringing back memories that were not really his, but recollections of the lives of others who had lived here, travelled here, and died long ago.

But there was something else too. He felt that their eyes were upon him, watching him, aware of his movements as he searched their land, and the feeling quickly became intense, the hairs at the nape of his neck rising involuntarily, so that he raised his head, jerking it around to look behind him. Then he turned slowly, to stare up at the windows at the rear of Deerbolt Hall.

From the corner of his eye he caught a quick movement. He looked directly up at the private apartments of David Gilmagesh and caught a brief glimpse of someone's face. It quickly dis-

116

appeared and Arnold grunted reflectively. So Sister Simone in her protective manner had lied to him: the leader of the cult of Oclixtan was present at the Hall – he merely did not wish to be bothered with any more interviews. Arnold continued to stare at the window, but the quick vision had gone, and for a moment Arnold wondered whether he had in fact seen anyone at all. He was reminded of the first time he had seen Gilmagesh, on the front steps of Deerbolt. He had seemed to be there, and yet was gone again in the blink of an eye. Just as he had seemed to disappear at the end of their interview in the heady, incense-laden dimness of the room.

Arnold shook his head. He was being foolish. This was all stock-in-trade for Gilmagesh: mystery, magic, sudden appearances and disappearances, shape-shifting travel into the cosmos. There would be a rational explanation for all of it, but Arnold wasn't going to waste time thinking about it. He had work to get on with in the fading light.

Armed with the survey map again he paced out the rectangular, raised areas outside the walls, measured the grass-covered, stony hummocks, and made notes on the possible locations of archaeologically interesting sites. Beneath what had once been the rear gate to Deerbolt Hall he found some evidence of a stone causeway: there had possibly been a small stream winding its way around past the rear of the Hall. It would bear investigation: he noted it on the survey map, pencilling it in with care. At last he looked about him, satisfied: the light was dying, and there was no more he could do. The next step would be to make out a report, requesting formal permission from David Gilmagesh, or Sister Simone, or whoever really was in charge, to undertake some exploratory digging, before Oclixtan decided to clamp down in the interests of secrecy.

The thought made him look up to the windows again: there was no movement this time, and he had no quick glimpse of a face, no raising of the hair at the back of his neck at the thought of some unseen watcher observing his activity. Smiling, Arnold shook his head, turned and began to walk back around the side of the building towards the main entrance, and the courtyard beyond.

The great doors in the gateway were still open, but as he

entered the courtyard he saw there was another car parked near his. And he heard voices raised, in altercation.

There were two men standing at the bottom of the steps to the main entrance. One, the stockier, more thick-set man, stood a little to one side, his body tense, his hands clenched and his whole attitude one of readiness, as though prepared to pounce quickly, and decisively. The other man, one foot on the second step, was extremely angry. He was slimmer, younger, and his arm was raised, gesticulating, his voice sharp and almost incoherent.

Facing them at the top of the steps was Sister Simone, and another smaller, slighter, cowled figure. As Arnold walked forward she seemed to shrink closer to the older woman, and a moment later he realised it was the acolyte Sister Simone had described as a submittor: the one named Sister Percepta.

As he approached, Sister Simone raised her head. Her hawkish features were set angrily, her eyes flashing with barely controlled fury. 'Mr Landon,' she called in an imperious tone. 'I require your assistance.'

The young man at the foot of the steps turned his head quickly. He stared at Arnold, his features flushed. 'Who the hell are you?' he snarled. 'Are you the one responsible for running this damned charade?'

His aggressive manner annoyed Arnold. He ignored him, as he approached the steps. 'What's the matter?' he asked quietly of Sister Simone.

She fixed him with a keen glance: there was no hint of fear in it. 'These men have forced themselves upon us here. I wish them to leave. They refuse to do so.'

Arnold nodded. He looked at the angry young man facing him; the other, heavier man was stepping forward quietly, in menacing support. 'This is private property. If Sister Simone wants you to leave –'

'Who the hell are you?'

'My name's Landon; I work for the authority at Morpeth –'

'A bloody *official*,' the young man sneered. 'Well, all this is nothing to do with you, so you'd be well advised to stay out of the way. I've come here to put an end to a bloody con trick, and end it I'm going to!'

118

He glared at Arnold for a few seconds and then, suddenly, catching them all off guard, he leapt up the remaining steps, pushed Sister Simone aside and grabbed the wrist of the younger woman. Off balance, Sister Percepta was dragged down the steps, stumbling as she came, until she fell, struggling, on her knees in the gravel of the courtyard. It happened quickly, before Arnold was able to react. He stepped forward, grabbing at the young man's arm, but as he did so the heavier, stockier man came forward swiftly and pinioned Arnold with thick-muscled arms. They stood there in a frozen tableau for a moment, Sister Percepta on her knees, crying out with pain and frustration, Sister Simone at the top of the steps, and Arnold pinned by the arms. He began to tense, ready to break free, but the arms holding him tightened their grip. 'Hold still, bonny lad,' the voice in his ear advised him, in a thick, grating tone. 'You could try stamping on my instep, or using your elbows, or trying to nut me across the nose, but I'm a canny street fighter, believe me, and if you don't behave yourself, you'll find yourself looking at a hospital ceiling!' There was a malicious chuckle. 'None of this is your business, so don't interfere. That there is Mr Colin Ledbury, and he's talking to his sister as he's every right to. I'm Jack Carter, his estate manager, along to make sure Mr Ledbury don't get interfered with when he's only acting within his rights. So let's stay quiet, and no one will get hurt.'

Sister Percepta was struggling to her feet. The cowl had fallen back from her head, and Arnold caught sight of her face: a young woman with dark-shadowed eyes, short black hair, a mouth twisted with panic and anger. She glared at the man holding her wrist. 'Let go of me, damn you! What are you trying to do?'

'I'm trying to make you see sense,' Colin Ledbury snapped. 'You're getting out of here ... you're coming home with me!'

'I'm doing no such thing!'

'They're holding you here against your will, Grace! You don't know what you're doing –'

'I know *exactly* what I'm doing! And I'm here because I *chose* to come here!'

Ledbury almost roared in frustration. 'Can't you see what this is all about? It's your bloody money they're after. All this damned foolishness – they've blinded you with their ridiculous talk of the other world just to get their hands on the estate.'

'If I choose to use my money in ways that suit me, that's nothing to do with you!' she cried, almost hysterical in her fear and anger. 'It's my money –'

'But they're using you –'

'And what are *you* trying to do?' she retorted, almost scream-ing. 'I don't know how you found me here, but I'm here because I'm fed up with being alone, fed up with you and your demands! It's you who's after my money, the money that Father left to me and not to you, because he knew that you'd squander it waste-fully, to support a lifestyle that's distasteful and criminal and low-life. He knew you're no good and would never do what's right. Well, I'm different: I know how to use the money properly, use it to seek after a higher truth, and there's nothing you can do about it! Now let me go!'

She half broke free from her brother, but he regained his grip on her wrist, swinging her back against him. Sister Simone started forward down the steps, determinedly, as Ledbury roared, 'I'll have you bloody committed to a mental home!' He raised his free hand as though to strike her and Arnold tensed, throwing himself forward, breaking free momentarily from Jack Carter's encircling grip. He tried to rush towards the struggling couple on the steps, but a blow took him on the shoulder and he was swung sideways. Carter, thick-set, an experienced street fighter, was facing him, half-crouching, a menacing glint in his eyes. His fingers were clenched, his fists balled. He appeared to be enjoying himself. 'I warned you, my friend. But if you want it, I'm happy to oblige . . .'

Arnold hesitated for a moment, one eye on the struggling brother and sister, one on the man facing him, and then, just as he was about to launch himself, beyond Carter he saw coming through the gate a long black Mercedes. He straightened, uncer-tain, and the man in front of him paused also. Sister Percepta turned her head, saw the car and immediately fell silent. As the car rasped over the gravel of the courtyard Sister Simone drew herself to her full height and was still, staring at the approaching vehicle as it whispered to a halt in front of them.

When the car engine died a silence swept over the courtyard.

It was as though they were in the eye of a storm, still, nothing moving and nothing alive. The man who stepped from the car had the dying afternoon light at his back, and his features seemed somehow blurred and indistinct in the growing dimness. It was as though he was of the twilight, protected by it, and he seemed to draw the silence about him like a cloak.

For a moment Arnold could not be sure, and then he realised it was David Gilmagesh. They stood there staring, as Gilmagesh, dressed completely in black – roll-necked sweater, trousers, shoes and hat – remained stock-still, watching them, his hands hanging limply by his side. There was something odd about his stance, and Arnold could not see his eyes, shadowed as they were by the wide-brimmed black hat. Worn by anyone else, Arnold would have seen it as a theatrical ostentation, but for Gilmagesh it seemed to add authority, mysticism to his bearing.

Colin Ledbury still held his sister's wrist but his fury was dissipating. Uncertainty crept into his eyes, but he held up his chin, raised a hand to point to Gilmagesh, realising who it was. 'You must be the guy behind all this crap! You'll be the one who's screwing my sister out of her inheritance and –'

Carter seemed to be frozen, staring back over his shoulder at the man in black, but the aggression was gone from his manner. He stood rigid, glaring at Gilmagesh, and then slowly seemed to come out of a trance. He moved quickly to Colin Ledbury's side and said something to him in a low, urgent voice.

Ledbury jerked away. 'What? Are you crazy?'

Carter's mouth was set grimly. He grabbed Ledbury's wrist, twisted it, pulled him away from his sister. 'This had better wait for another day. I think we'd better leave. Now!'

Half-dazed and uncomprehending, Colin Ledbury allowed himself to be pulled away, half-dragged towards their car. Sister Percepta – Grace Ledbury, Arnold now knew – was crying, running up the steps back into the Hall. Sister Simone stood stock-still, staring at David Gilmagesh as he walked quietly forward, holding her with his cold, contemptuous glance. At the foot of the steps he looked at Arnold, but there was no sign, no gesture of recognition: it was as though they had never met, and as though he did not really see him even now. Then without saying a word Gilmagesh walked up the steps past Sister Simone and into the Hall.

Sister Simone remained where she was, watching as Colin Ledbury and his estate manager drove out of the courtyard. When the sound of the car engine faded, she looked at Arnold stony-featured, but she said nothing. Sheepishly, Arnold decided this was not a good time to talk with her or Gilmagesh about the site outside the walls of Deerbolt Hall.

He went back to his car. As he drove away through the tree-lined avenue he puzzled about the impact the arrival of Gilmagesh seemed to have had on the events in the courtyard: it was as though for some inexplicable reason Jack Carter had suddenly been scared out of his wits.

But it was only as Arnold reached Morpeth in the gathering gloom that he realised Sister Simone had told the truth: David Gilmagesh had been away from Deerbolt Hall. In which case, Arnold wondered, who had been watching him earlier, from the windows of the Shaman's private apartment?

3

Late the following week Arnold still had not telephoned Jane. He could not quite explain his reluctance, even to himself. As far as their relationship was concerned, she had always said he was indecisive, unable to demonstrate the kind of commitment she desired. And perhaps she was right, because he had the feeling that once he made the call it would be the end – or the beginning – of something. And he was still torn, uncertain what answer he should give to Professor Schwartz.

He had made a written report to Karen Stannard, recommending the department should make a start on the work at Deerbolt Hall, but making no reference to the scene he had witnessed between Ledbury and the women of Oclixtan. She did not get back to him for several days, and he saw nothing of her nor of Portia Tyrrel as he took the opportunity to visit some of the digs that he was supervising on behalf of the department in the hills inland from Rothbury. They had been partly financed by English Heritage and by the University of Newcastle, but Arnold held a watching brief, and his assistance had been called on several times as they considered some of the artefacts recovered from what seemed to be a Saxon burial site. When he returned to Morpeth on Thursday evening he found a note on his desk to say that he was called to a meeting at eight on Friday evening. A representative of Oclixtan would be in attendance.

Arnold caught up with his paperwork during Friday. There was a Museums Committee meeting at six, but his presence was not required: it was one of the tasks delegated to Portia Tyrrel. But she was waiting when Arnold made his way to Karen Stannard's room shortly before eight o'clock.

The two women seemed at ease with each other when Arnold entered. They had probably come to some kind of accommodation in their relationship: the edginess Arnold had earlier observed seemed to have dissipated, for the time being at least. It augured well for the working atmosphere.

Karen waved him to a seat and fixed him with a friendly glance. 'Thank you for your report, Arnold. It gives me useful background. I phoned the people at Deerbolt earlier in the week ... Sister Simone, was it? Anyway, when I explained what we had decided to do, she said she'd try to arrange a meeting.'

'So you've reached a decision?'

'Based on your recommendation, of course,' she replied with a hint of irony. 'It's supported by Portia. I've decided I can find sufficient funds in the departmental budget to make a start, and it seems to me we ought to do just that ... if only to assert our interest.'

The telephone on her desk buzzed. She picked it up, listened for a moment and then nodded. 'Send him up.' She looked at Arnold and Portia and smiled. 'It seems we're being honoured by a visit from the man himself.'

David Gilmagesh entered the room a few minutes later. He came forward, ignoring Arnold and Portia, and introduced himself to Karen Stannard. He held her glance, and her hand, a few seconds longer than she had anticipated and for almost the first time in his experience Arnold saw that Karen seemed somewhat flustered. A slight colour came to her cheeks under the directness

123

of the man's gaze, and her tongue flickered over dry lips as she turned to introduce him to Arnold and Portia.

'But we've already met,' Gilmagesh announced, favouring Portia with a languid smile, and Arnold with a quick, dismissive glance and nod of the head.

'Of course,' Karen replied and waved him to a seat. Arnold watched him as he moved the chair so that he could see all three of them. He was dressed in black again, but was hatless on this occasion. His face seemed thinner than Arnold recalled, his blond hair was carefully brushed back from his forehead, and there was a whipcord leanness about his frame that Arnold had not observed earlier.

'How is Sister Percepta?' Arnold asked, leaning forward.

The ice-blue eyes regarded him blankly for several seconds. Then they seemed to film over reflectively, before he answered. 'She is well, of course. Her ordination will take place soon.'

Arnold was aware of Karen Stannard's inquisitively raised eyebrow. She would be wondering who Sister Percepta might be.

'Will the ordination be in your new chapel?' Portia asked. She flicked a quick, mischievous glance in Arnold's direction and he knew she'd be thinking of the antics of the Agapemone.

David Gilmagesh was silent for a little while. 'The work is not yet finished,' he said at last. 'But it is possible.'

'And there's been no more trouble?' Arnold asked.

Gilmagesh regarded him. There was a cold, vague light in his eyes and his mouth was hard. 'Trouble?' He shook his head slowly, his glance still fixed on Arnold. 'Oclixtan is largely impervious to the outside world and matters of no consequence are . . . of no consequence. But I am here in response to your call to Sister Simone. I thought it best to come myself to meet you, so there can be no misunderstandings in any agreement we reach.'

'I'm sure there won't be,' Karen Stannard intervened briskly. 'And I'm glad you've been able to find time to come along to see us. I'm sorry it's so late in the evening, but committee work –'

'What exactly is it that you're planning to do?' Gilmagesh interrupted.

Karen Stannard paused, and then looked at Arnold, raised an elegantly arched eyebrow, inviting him to respond.

124

'We'd like to begin a survey of the area outside your private apartments, extending down towards the reconstruction work you're doing on your ... ah ... chapel. There's a view that the ancient drovers' track ended in some medieval structures, and there's a causeway that I think we should be looking at –'

'May I see some plans of what you have in mind?'

Karen Stannard opened the folder in front of her and turned it, so that Gilmagesh was able to see the neatly outlined plans of the area Arnold had mentioned. Gilmagesh pored over it for a little while, as Karen explained the plans to him, a slim, carefully manicured nail tracing the outline of the projected work. Arnold contented himself with observing Gilmagesh. This was the third time he had met him now, and he was left with the fanciful notion that each time they met there was a subtle change in the man's appearance. It was nothing Arnold could put a finger on, and the three meetings had of course been under entirely different circumstances: the dim recesses of Deerbolt Hall, the gathering twilight of the courtyard, and now in Karen Stannard's brightly lit office. But there were moments when Arnold felt he was looking at someone he had never met before. His mind began to range over the occasion of their first meeting, and he seemed to sense again the heady, incense-heavy air, and hear the claims of the acolyte and the shaman himself, the flight to the cosmos, the shape-shifting, the descent to the underworld ...

'How long would you be expecting to take in completing this work?'

Arnold was jerked back to the present. Portia Tyrrel was looking at him with amusement in her eyes. 'Ah ... it's difficult to say,' he stammered. 'Perhaps three weeks, depending on what manpower we can assign to the project –'

'That would be out of the question,' Gilmagesh asserted firmly.

Karen Stannard's tone was cool. She leaned forward, one finger caressing the line of her perfectly formed lips. 'The previous owner of Deerbolt made a commitment –'

'I cannot be responsible for the commitments of the previous owner,' Gilmagesh interrupted. 'This is an important time for Oclixtan. We have been established here now for two years or more, and our influence is growing. But such growth demands our own kind of . . . commitments. And we cannot permit the interference of the outside world. Privacy is essential.'

'We wouldn't be interfering with –'

'I came here myself tonight because I felt it necessary I should meet you and explain. We are reaching a critical time in the development of Oclixtan: we are reaching out to the mysteries of the cosmos and external demands must be resisted. I am aware of other arrangements you have made. But we shall be sealing Oclixtan within the month. So, if you desire to undertake any work it must be done quickly. By the time the new moon rises our preparations must be completed. After that, we shall be closing our gates, sealing our boundaries, and with the sisters I shall be undertaking the first of our spiritual ascents . . .'

It had become almost a chant. Arnold stared at Gilmagesh: the man's eyes seemed glazed, and yet Arnold had the feeling that nothing Gilmagesh would say or do would be spontaneous. Even now, though the words he used were ridiculous, and designed for a very different audience to the one in front of him, he was confident enough to use them, and was aware of their effect. They were all silent for a few moments.

Arnold cleared his throat. 'I can understand your need for privacy, but I'm not sure –'

Gilmagesh turned cold eyes on him. 'The situation is not negotiable, Mr Landon. Oclixtan owns the property: it is private land. Your department has no rights over the land – your presence there would be only under our licence. And that means . . . the end of the month. After that, we would regard you as trespassers.'

There seemed little more to be said. The meeting continued in a subdued form for another half-hour or so, as Karen half-heartedly argued for a longer access period, but by nine o'clock it was clear that there was no way forward other than to agree to Gilmagesh's conditions. He left, sweeping out majestically, proceeding almost silently along the corridor.

'Bloody charlatan,' Karen Stannard said with contempt in her voice.

The following Monday afternoon Arnold finally got around to

126

putting in a call to the States. He had meant to do it over the weekend but somehow had been reluctant; at four in the afternoon he eventually used his personal mobile to call Jane's apartment in New York. He got the answering machine: she was not available. He considered the matter and then looked in his wallet for the card Professor Schwartz had given him. There was the possibility that Jane might be at the university in New Mexico.

When the university switchboard finally put Arnold through, Schwartz's voice sounded deep, and somewhat tired, but there was a genuine pleasure in his tone. 'Landon! It's good to hear from you – we were only talking about you at the weekend.'

Arnold hesitated. 'Ah . . . so I guess Jane is down there with you. I'd tried her apartment in New York . . .'

'Aw, she's been here at the university for this last week or so. But if you're hoping to have a word with her, I'm afraid you've just missed her. She's on her way back east – I saw her off at the airport just an hour ago. Say, how are things with you?'

'Fine . . . and the dig in the Mojave desert?'

'It's proceeding well enough, though we've not turned up anything startling. That was what we were talking about, Jane and I . . . the kind of luck you seem to carry around with you. We could sure use some of it out here right now. Have you reached a decision yet, about the offer I made?'

A strange note of caution seemed to have entered his voice. 'I can't say I have,' Arnold replied. 'I appreciate the opportunity, but things have been pretty active here and I just don't seem . . .'

There was a short pause, then Schwartz's voice crackled back. 'Well, the sooner you make up your mind, Arnold, the better. You'll appreciate it's not an offer I can keep open indefinitely. I'm in sore need of a research assistant, and, well, you know how it is.' He paused, and then went on, 'I think Jane really would like to see you out here.'

The caution was very noticeable, Arnold thought. He began to wonder whether his presence in New Mexico would really be as appreciated by Schwartz as the man suggested. He told the professor he understood his position, and promised to let him have a decision soon. Meanwhile, he'd probably leave it to the next day before he tried to contact Jane again, to give her time to get back to New York. Schwartz agreed – 'I tell you, the traffic into the city these days is murder' – and was about to ring off, when a sudden thought struck Arnold.

'Ah . . . just one second, Professor Schwartz –'

'The name's Don.'

'Ah . . . yes, Don . . . I was just wondering . . . I seem to recall when I visited you in the Mojave, and we were discussing the shaman tomb, you said you'd been bothered by some cult that had sprung up near the site. You'd ended up writing some kind of article about the man who ran it . . .'

'Oh, yeah, that's right. He left here couple of years back, not long after my exposé. There was a bit of a row about my article at the time, and it caused some friction between the shaman and his apologist, the guy who did most of the writing up of his exploits. I think they sort of fell out, in fact – I got the impression the guy wanted rather more recognition for his work than the shaman was prepared to allow. But, unsurprisingly, their own quarrel seemed to get patched up once the IRS investigation started and they certainly skedaddled together once the IRS people got after them. They vanished quick enough when tax officers started asking questions.'

'What was his name?'

'The shaman? Huh . . . What was it, now . . .? Barton, that was it. He and his sidekick, they worked closely together until their quarrel and after that the cult was somewhat undermined. But I got a contact in the IRS, nephew of mine in fact, and he told me he thought Barton had got right out of the jurisdiction, with his friend in tow.'

'What did he look like?' Arnold asked curiously.

'Barton? Tallish, lean face, fair hair. Funny kind of eyes . . . But I only met him a few times. Why do you ask?'

Arnold hesitated. 'I'm not sure, really, but we've got some kind of shamanic cult starting up here, in our area. It's just that some of the things he and his acolytes have been saying, they remind me of comments you made when we met in the Mojave. There's been talk of the *nagual*, and I've seen him wearing a robe with a jaguar motif . . . And there's the suggestion that maybe

128

people are handing over money to accompany him on his so-called trips to the cosmos . . .'

Don Schwartz laughed, a deep rumble of cynical amusement. 'Sounds like you got one just like ours . . . or are you suggesting maybe we're talking about the same guy?'

'I don't really know. But the physical description . . . It sounds similar. The name's not the same. The man who claims to be a shaman here calls himself Gilmagesh –'

'Oh, our friend out here didn't use his real name, Barton – he had some fancy shamanic name he used with his followers. No, I wouldn't be surprised if it's the same guy. Is this important?'

Arnold hesitated. 'I don't suppose it is, really. I mean, it's nothing to do with me or my work here at the department except that we're getting somewhat involved with the cult he's started. But it's always helpful to have some sort of background, when you deal with people like David Gilmagesh.'

'Yeah, that's right . . .' There was a short pause. 'I just wonder whether it could be the same guy . . . As far as I recall, he sort of skipped quickly, did an overnight flit, him and his buddy. But I think maybe I'll have a word with my nephew again, see if he's got any further information.'

'I don't want to put you to any trouble.'

'Naw, forget it, I'd be happy to take a look. The bastard gave me enough trouble here in the Mojave, and I'd be interested to find out whether there's any chance it's the same guy who's crossed your path there in England . . . I'll be in touch, hey?'

'I'm grateful,' Arnold said.

After he had switched off the phone Arnold sat thinking about Jane Wilson. It was clear she was spending more and more time away from New York, working with Don Schwartz in the Mojave, and maybe that was why she hadn't got in touch with Arnold. Or maybe both Arnold and Jane were somehow seeking time and distance to get their own thoughts into order. He checked his watch. He'd do as he had suggested, and perhaps leave it until the next day before he tried to contact her again in New York.

He gathered up some files he had to return to the archives and made his way to the door. As he stepped into the corridor he sighed: Jerry Picton was lounging his way towards him. The mean, weaselly features of the office gossip lit up as Picton saw Arnold: he stopped in front of him, almost barring his way.

'Arnold! So how are things going on between you and the little Chinese cracker?'

'She's Singaporean,' Arnold growled.

'Whatever.' Jerry Picton grinned, showing his green teeth. 'I was talking to her this morning about that Colonel McArdle business. I haven't heard whether the police have picked up anything more about it all, but you and the Portia lady had had dinner with him not long before he died, hadn't you?'

'That's right,' Arnold replied and tried to edge his way past the man.

'And now there's another one,' Picton said as Arnold managed to make his way down the corridor.

Arnold paused as the comment hit home. He stopped, looked back at Jerry Picton. 'What do you mean?'

'Since McArdle,' Picton replied, cocking his head on one side conspiratorially. 'He'd been up in arms about something connected with the Ridgeway estate, hadn't he? I was talking to Fred Orrell and he said you'd been to see him . . .'

'But what do you mean, another one?'

Picton grinned unpleasantly. 'Haven't you heard? There's been a buzz around Morpeth about it. That guy . . . the son of the old man who owned the Ridgeway estate. Orrell tells me he was trying to do some deal over building developments, and McArdle was arguing with him about land, and then McArdle died . . .'

'Well?'

'So now it's Ledbury's turn.'

'How do you mean?'

'Seems they found young Ledbury in a back street in North Shields on Friday evening. Knife in his gut.' Jerry Picton flashed his green teeth in a malicious grin. 'You get involved with the strangest people, don't you, Arnold?'

PART FIVE

1

Culpeper regretted that the matter of the death of Colin Ledbury had fallen within his jurisdiction, not least because it had brought the task force back into his office. They sat there hungrily, O'Connor, Farnsby, Garcia, regarding him like eager wolves, waiting for some tasty titbit to be thrown to them. Culpeper was annoyed. He already had enough on his plate without having to listen to their theories about a mysterious stranger on Tyneside.

'So what brings the triumvirate to my office again?' Culpeper rumbled.

Farnsby bobbed his head, glancing quickly at his companions. 'We thought it might be useful to give you a progress report on our investigation, and we wondered whether you'd managed to pick up anything about the Ledbury killing on Monday night.'

'Now why would you be interested in the murder of Colin Ledbury?'

There was a short pause. O'Connor leaned forward, his saturnine features calm, but his eyes sharp as he stared at Culpeper. 'We feel there may be some link to our investigations.'

'Such as?'

'The possibility that the killing was drug-related.'

'And what makes you suppose it might have been?'

O'Connor shrugged casually. 'The contacts you gave us . . . they've been useful. The rumour along the river is that there was some kind of link between Ledbury's estate manager –'

'Carter,' Culpeper supplied.

'– and what's been happening recently in Newcastle and Teesport.'

Culpeper sighed theatrically. 'All right, let's begin with what *has* been happening. And then we can discuss the possible links. Fire away.'

It was Inspector Garcia who began. Earnestly, with his dark, intelligent eyes fixed on Culpeper, he said, 'We now have confirmation from the European networks that a new system is being established along the north-east entry points. Interpol has been able to identify a route that begins, as usual, in South-East Asia, but the European off-loading takes place in the Spanish possession in Morocco – Ceuta. It's a swift crossing from there into northern Spain, and we have reports of activity that is bypassing the Barcelona clearing house.'

'It looks as though a new supply route has been set up from Santander,' O'Connor added. 'It runs in through a network that's been set up at Teesside, and ultimately Newcastle. And we're fairly certain that's where our friend Jordan fits in. The snouts you gave us . . . they've not been able to point a finger, or lead us to him, but the rumours along the river suggest that there's someone new setting all this up.'

'And we think it's Jordan.'

'Our theory,' Farnsby added, nodding in agreement with Garcia, 'is that Jordan came over from the States when he heard that Timothy Brazil was milking the system, cutting out some of the profits for himself. Brazil heard that the syndicate was after him and intended going to ground but Jordan took him on the *Dawn Princess*, disposed of him, then returned to Barcelona to smooth things over with the distributors there, before flying to Newcastle to set up a new distribution system in northern England.'

'But you haven't been able to get a fix on Jordan yet?'

There was a short silence. 'He keeps his tracks well covered,' O'Connor said at last.

Culpeper scowled and shook his head. 'I don't know why you think I can help in any of this. I've got more than enough to get on with already. Colonel McArdle tumbles from the bell tower at his manor house and there's suspicious circumstances there; Colin Ledbury gets knifed in an alley in North Shields and I've got to look into that as well, short-staffed as I already am.' He glared at Farnsby, who wriggled uncomfortably under the implied criticism. 'So why you think I can find time to help your task force, I can't imagine.'

'This man Carter . . . we hear he's had connections with the trade along the river,' O'Connor said quietly.

Culpeper fixed him with a cool glance. 'Carter is a roustabout.

He's had a finger in a number of criminal pies over the years. He's been a muscle man in the main: an enforcer. Yes, he has been known to have connections of the kind you suggest, but –'

'And Colin Ledbury has been involved in the drug scene in London,' O'Connor interrupted.

Culpeper considered the matter coolly. At last, he admitted, 'Yes, that's so.'

'What precisely do we know about Ledbury's death?' O'Connor asked.

'No witnesses, of course,' Culpeper replied sourly. 'His body was found in an alleyway, not far from the night-club near the front at Shields. We've got an estimated time of death: about eight thirty on Friday evening. There were no signs of a struggle: there had been one blow from a sharp-bladed instrument. Pierced his lung and stomach. He died painfully.'

'And probably noisily,' O'Connor mused. 'Yet no witnesses.'

'North Shields folk aren't inclined to muck about in other people's business,' Culpeper suggested sourly. 'I've no doubt someone will have heard the scuffling – maybe the person who put in the anonymous phone call to report the body. But we've got no names.'

'But you don't think this killing is drug-related? You don't think it has anything to do with the presence of Charlie Jordan on Tyneside?' O'Connor insisted.

'I'm not aware you've *evidence* yet that this man Jordan actually is on Tyneside! And I see no connection established between Ledbury and Jordan.'

'Carter?' Inspector Garcia pressed.

Culpeper wriggled in annoyance. His heavy brows drew together. 'I . . . I'm not convinced there is a link as you suggest. I'm following a different line of enquiry at the moment. As for Carter . . . well, he seems to have done a runner.'

'Well, doesn't that suggest –'

'It suggests to me that he may well have put the knife in himself,' Culpeper said angrily. 'Or that he's gone into hiding because he knows things that he doesn't want to tell us. But either way, I'm not convinced it has anything to do with your

135

damned Jordan and his supposed drug distribution ring. And I've got more urgent calls on my time –'

'So what is the line of enquiry you're following?' O'Connor asked quietly.

Culpeper hesitated. He looked at Farnsby, as though this interrogation was all his fault. Then he shrugged. There seemed no reason why he shouldn't tell them.

It had been Arnold Landon who had set the hare running.

He had come voluntarily to the headquarters at Ponteland to see Culpeper. He had seemed edgy, somewhat nervous, perhaps concerned that he might be offering useless information, or pointing the finger at an innocent party. Culpeper knew him to be a man of principle, and disinclined to gossip.

'So what's it all about?' Culpeper had asked.

'The killing of Colin Ledbury.'

'You know something about it?'

Landon had shaken his head doubtfully. 'Not really. But . . . you're still looking into the death of Colonel McArdle, aren't you?'

'We are,' Culpeper said carefully, 'but what's that got to do with Ledbury?'

Landon had wrinkled his brow in concern. 'I'm not at all certain, really, but it's just the coincidence . . .'

'Tell me.'

'Well, there's a sort of link between McArdle and Ledbury. There was an argument running between them, of course, a boundary dispute.'

'We know about that. Ledbury had an involvement with a building consortium, and he wanted that strip of land. So . . .?'

Landon sighed uncertainly. 'I can't quite get things straight in my mind, but apart from the argument between McArdle and Ledbury, both of them also seemed to be involved in . . . well, a relationship with the owners of Deerbolt Hall.'

'What do you mean, a *relationship*?' Culpeper had asked slowly.

'McArdle had made a complaint against the cult which has been established at Deerbolt. It calls itself Oclixtan, and it's led by a man known as David Gilmagesh. They've been carrying out some development work on site, and McArdle's antiquarian interests had caused him to complain to Morpeth, ask for action to be taken.'

'So what's that got to do with Colin Ledbury?'

'Nothing, of course. But Ledbury also had a problem with Oclixtan.'

'In what way?'

'I was up there the other day . . . late last week. I was witness to a . . . dispute.'

'What happened?'

Landon shrugged vaguely. 'There was a shouting match. Ledbury and a man called Carter were there. It seems Colin Ledbury was trying to . . . persuade his sister to leave the cult, and return to her home –'

'His sister? *Grace* Ledbury?'

'That's right.' Landon had paused, puzzled by Culpeper's reaction. 'Do you know her?'

Culpeper shook his head. 'No, but Ledbury had asked us to look for her. Now it seems he found her without our help.' So that was where she had got to, he thought to himself. Running away from her brother and his demands for money, running away to the sanctuary of a cult . . . 'Hmm. All right. Go on.'

'Well, that was about it, really.'

'That was all?' Culpeper had frowned. 'An altercation? There was nothing else?'

Unhappily, Landon had admitted, 'There was a bit of pushing and shoving went on. I got . . . involved somewhat with Carter, but when Gilmagesh turned up everything seemed to . . . sort of collapse. But I thought you ought to know, at least . . . well, when I heard about Ledbury's death –'

'You thought we should be informed there'd been a bit of a barney between Colin Ledbury and this Gilmagesh character.' Culpeper watched Landon carefully. 'So do you think this dispute over Grace Ledbury might have provided sufficient motive for someone to kill Colin Ledbury?'

'I hardly think that! I mean, a dispute over whether his sister should remain in Oclixtan, even if a lot of money was involved ... and besides, if the reports of Ledbury's death are accurate –'

'What do you mean?'

'He died on Friday evening, I understand. In North Shields.'

Culpeper nodded. 'That's so. About eight thirty.'

'David Gilmagesh was at our Morpeth headquarters until nine o'clock that evening. So he couldn't have been involved ...'

When Culpeper had repeated the gist of his conversation with Arnold Landon to the task force in his office a silence fell. At last O'Connor cleared his throat and said, 'Let's get this clear ... The line of enquiry you're following involves this ... cult called ...'

'Oclixtan.'

'I don't follow the relationships.'

Culpeper sighed. 'Neither do I, really. There's a sort of triangle I haven't worked out yet. Colonel McArdle is upset with Ledbury over a boundary, and with Gilmagesh over antiquarian matters. He dies. Ledbury's man Carter has arguments with McArdle; Ledbury and Carter have a dispute with Gilmagesh over Ledbury's sister and then Ledbury is killed –'

'At least you can close the Grace Ledbury enquiry,' Farnsby muttered.

Culpeper glared at him. He had never devoted much manpower to that search in any case, and Farnsby knew it. 'We're looking for Carter, of course. It may well be he's the key to all this. It's possible that Ledbury's murder was just a matter of employer and employee falling out. We'll know more when we get hold of Carter. But I think you'll begin to appreciate that at the moment there's no clear line that leads to anyone. And as for your man –'

'Charlie Jordan,' Inspector Garcia said thoughtfully.

'Well, I don't see where he fits into any of the picture at all. So this meeting is a waste of time. You've got your job to do – find this Jordan character. Me, I've got to find out who killed Colonel McArdle, and who stuck a knife into Colin Ledbury. The one thing we can be sure of, however, is that this crackerbarrel

138

Gilmagesh didn't do it. He's got an alibi for the time Ledbury died, and there's never been a suggestion he went near McArdle's house. So, can we go our separate ways, gentlemen? Do our own thing, so to speak?'

Garcia, Farnsby and O'Connor rose to their feet as Culpeper began to shuffle papers on his desk, impatiently. O'Connor watched him for a few seconds, and then smiled grimly. 'You remind me of my old man,' he said.

Culpeper raised his head. 'I hope that's to be taken as a compliment,' he glowered.

O'Connor hesitated, then grimaced. 'Maybe so. He was an old-fashioned copper too.'

The door closed quietly behind them.

It was perhaps an hour later that there was a tap on the door. When Culpeper called out, Inspector Farnsby entered. He stood there in front of his senior officer, uncomfortable, but with a determined glint in his eyes.

'Well?'

Farnsby shuffled, locked his hands behind his back and met Culpeper's glare stubbornly. 'I didn't want to say anything in front of the others, sir. It would have been disloyal.'

Culpeper snorted. He wasn't aware that he had ever demanded loyalty from the Chief Constable's blue-eyed boy – or expected it.

Doggedly, Farnsby went on. 'It's the manner in which you dismissed any connection with the Jordan matter, sir.'

'I don't see any.'

'I'm not so sure that's an accurate statement, sir.'

Culpeper leaned back in his chair, raised an interrogative eyebrow and regarded Farnsby with distaste. 'You got something on your chest, bonny lad. Better get it off before it chokes you.'

Farnsby raised his chin defiantly. 'I'll begin by saying that I've not been prying, sir; I've not been interfering in an investigation that you've been conducting.'

'The investigations I've been conducting *should* have involved you, Farnsby. Better that, than have you pussyfooting around with an Irishman and a Spaniard!'

Ignoring the jibe, Farnsby ploughed on. 'You say there's no

139

link that you can see between the enquiries carried out by the task force, and your own. But that's not what I hear, sir. Information has come to me –'

'Oh, yes,' Culpeper interrupted sarcastically. 'Are we talking station gossip here?'

'I was talking to the liaison officer yesterday,' Farnsby went on stubbornly. 'He tells me you've had a report from Forensic concerning the death of Colonel McArdle.'

'I have,' Culpeper replied contemplatively.

'I'm told there were traces of drugs in McArdle's body, sir. Now if that's the case, it seems to me there's a clear link between what the task force is looking at and –'

'Farnsby,' Culpeper interrupted with a measured patience in his tone. 'The drug trade along the river . . . what sort of drugs are we talking about?'

'Well, sir, the usual stuff. Cannabis, ecstasy, crack, heroin, cocaine, smack – there's a whole range . . .'

'Peyote?'

'Sir?'

'You didn't mention peyote. I mean, I imagine there must be a roaring trade in that stuff. It's got to be the latest thrill out there, the pill all the youngsters are popping at the old warehouse raves down by the docks. I mean, there *must* be regular runners in the West End; a demand for supplies along the river . . .' Culpeper's tone was heavy with sarcasm. 'The task force must have come across some information about this new trip, this new fix that's suddenly become available to the blasé users from Meadowwell . . .'

Stiffly, Farnsby said, 'You told the others that you saw no connection with the Jordan enquiry, but traces of a drug were found in McArdle's body. I just feel it would have been more appropriate if *all* information were made available to everyone involved in these parallel investigations –'

'Parallel investigations, my backside! Farnsby, you're out of line. You carry on playing your games with O'Connor and Garcia, sucking up to the Chief Constable, but I've no time for all that. I'll just tell you this. I see no connection between your Jordan manhunt and the traces we found in McArdle. This isn't a commercial drug we're talking about: it's not something that's commonly traded. It's something that comes from an hallucin-ogenic plant – the peyote cactus. I don't see too many of *those* growing along the Tyne Valley or in the hills of Northumberland. It's a psychotropic plant the essence of which is known to medical science: indeed, it seems that occasionally it is taken by both doctor and patient, in a curing session to wean an addict off the drug, so that they have a shared field of vision. Sounds crazy to me, but there you are, I'm just a simple copper. But the point I'm making, Farnsby, is that I don't see any market for peyote among the distribution network in the north-east. That's why I didn't mention it to your friends. That's why I consider it of no consequence to your investigations. To raise it as an issue would only confuse matters; muddy the waters.'

He held Farnsby's glance and shook his head. 'No, you just plod quietly along with your bloody task force and let me get on with my work. And when you've been relieved of that duty, then you can come along here and question my methods and my information release.'

If you've got the temerity to do that, he thought to himself as he watched the slow flush staining Farnsby's neck. But the younger man was still not finished. 'I take it, however, that you won't object if I pass this information on to O'Connor and Garcia, sir.'

'In that respect, you can do what you bloody well like, Farnsby. But don't step on my toes . . .'

After Farnsby had gone Culpeper sat staring out of the win-dow for a little while, thinking the matter over. He wondered whether there was anything in what the younger man had told him. O'Connor had said he was an old-fashioned copper. He'd probably meant that Culpeper was the kind of stubborn, narrow-minded, fixated policeman of the old school who would dog-gedly resist new ideas and reject criticism or contributions from younger officers.

It wasn't all that long now to retirement, thank God. But maybe there was something in what Farnsby had said – not that Culpeper was going to admit that to the arrogant young bastard. Still . . . perhaps he'd better have another word about the Oclixtan cult with Arnold Landon . . .

141

It would take a while to be able to bring together a small team to carry out the investigation of the Deerbolt Hall site as Karen Stannard had suggested, but Arnold was hopeful that it could be done faster than anticipated: a visit to the university at Newcastle resulted in a promise that a number of researchers would be found from among third-year students. They would not be available for another week or so, however, so he decided it would be sensible if he himself undertook some of the preliminary work in mapping the site more carefully. He explained to Karen Stannard, and suggested that it might be useful if Portia Tyrrel were to join him.

The silence that followed the suggestion was freezing. He gained the clear impression that Karen did not want him to spend too much time with her assistant. Arnold suspected she was fearful that they might in some way become close enough to undermine her as acting head of the department; on the other hand, he had seen the manner in which they could occasionally behave almost like a couple of schoolgirls, giggling over private jokes. He found it difficult to weigh up Portia but he suspected she had her own agenda, and it might not be one which coexisted easily with that of Karen Stannard herself.

So he made his way to Deerbolt Hall in the bright mid-morning sunshine, alone, after a brief visit to the office. He enjoyed the drive, as he always did when he ventured into the hills of Northumberland: the sweep of the fells was outlined in a hazy blue, and the air was clean and invigorating, with the hint of salt in his nostrils as the breeze swept in from the distant sea.

The gates to Deerbolt Hall were closed when he arrived, the heavy, dark, iron-riveted wood presenting a formidable, secretive face to the outside world. Arnold parked his car just outside the gates, took out a small haversack and walked around the side of the hall, clambering over the bank towards the old drovers' way and heading towards the rear of the house. He glanced towards the rise of the hill, and the clump of woodland at its crest. It was near lunchtime; he'd brought some sandwiches with him and after a brief hesitation he decided to walk along the drovers' track towards the woods. It was up there that Colonel McArdle had stationed himself to watch what was happening in Oclixtan . . .

The track rose gently, swinging to accommodate the steepening rise and folds of the land, and skirted the edge of the woods. Arnold paused and looked back: Deerbolt Hall lay below him, bathed in sunshine, and he could clearly see the roof where the construction work was being carried out, now all but completed. He also had a clear view into the windows of the private apartment used by David Gilmagesh, but from this distance there was nothing to be seen of the rooms themselves. The colonel had, of course, carried binoculars.

At the edge of the woods, hidden from the house, Arnold came across an overgrown, ancient quarry. He paused there, looking down the steep cliff that fell away below him, wondering how old the scar on the landscape might be. It was more than likely the quarry would have been used to provide stone for the building of Deerbolt Hall but there was also the possibility that it would have been the supply source for much older constructions along the drovers' track. To the left of the quarry the trees grew almost to its edge and Arnold made his way across there, sat down with his back to an ancient oak, and opened the haversack to take out his package of sandwiches. He sat there eating his lunch, head back, enjoying the sunshine on his face.

He had been there for some twenty minutes, and was half dozing when he heard a scuttling sound. He opened his eyes and then sat without moving as he saw a fox slipping out of the woods to the edge of the quarry. It made its way across the clearing in front of him, oblivious to his presence. Then it must have caught his scent for it paused, turned its head and caught sight of him, motionless under the oak tree. It froze, one foot raised, and stood there for a while, staring at him curiously, unafraid. It was a dog fox, its reddish fur burning in the sun, its head held low as it regarded him. Then, after a little while, it turned its head quickly, glanced away from him and slipped over the edge of the quarry on some unseen path, out of sight. Something had disturbed the animal: Arnold glanced to his right and saw the woman.

She had come up the same path that Arnold had used. She was standing at the edge of the quarry, dressed in the robes affected by the sisters of Oclixtan, staring down into the drop in front of her. She was motionless, and presented an almost eerie figure in the surrounding silence. Arnold sat still, observing her. After a little while she turned away from the cliff edge and began to pace towards him, her head bent, hands buried in the sleeves of her robe, like a medieval nun lost in prayerful meditation.

She was only ten feet from him when she became aware of his presence. She stopped, looked up, and Arnold scrambled to his feet. 'I'm sorry,' he said quickly. 'I hope I didn't alarm you.'

She stared at him for a moment, then pushed back her cowl. It was Sister Percepta. 'What are you doing up here?' she asked.

Arnold shrugged, managed a smile. 'Having my lunch, before doing some work down below.'

'You've been here to Oclixtan before. You're Mr Landon. You were here the other day, when Colin . . .'

He nodded; hesitated. Her eyes were red-rimmed, her face pale and drawn and he guessed she had been crying. 'I . . . I'm sorry to hear about your brother.'

She stared at him vacantly for several seconds, then inclined her head slightly. 'They only told me this morning. That he was dead. They didn't tell me how he died. Sister Simone . . . she reiterated that our duty is to seek the transformation of the other self, and it can only be achieved by relinquishing the ties of blood and family and the outside world. I should feel no grief . . . and yet . . . How *did* he die, Mr Landon?'

Arnold hesitated. He was reluctant to speak, concerned that he might upset her further. 'I'm not sure . . . It could have been an accident. He was found in North Shields,' he said lamely.

Sister Percepta regarded him gravely for a little while. He guessed she knew he was lying, but she made no attempt to cross-question him. 'I remember him as a child,' she said. 'But he

144

changed. We weren't close . . . none of us were in the family. We went our own ways. But when my father died, and I returned, all I wanted was peace but my brother wouldn't leave me alone, pestered me, wanting money, always money . . .' She looked about her, vaguely. 'Here is peace. In Oclixtan there is peace, and the reality of the true self, with the whole of the world to roam . . .'

She stopped, and turned to stare across the quarry to where the land fell away, a distant view to the far blue hills. After a moment, Arnold asked, 'Will you stay with Oclixtan now?'

'Since my brother is dead?' She seemed to regard the question as foolish. 'Of course. His death is an irrelevance. Here is my home. I need nothing except Oclixtan, nothing of the world. With David Gilmagesh I shall fly . . .'

She began to walk away, slowly, then she stopped, looked back to him, stared at him for several seconds. 'He should not have come,' she said. 'He should not have come looking for me.'

Arnold watched her as she walked back, skirting the woods, along the drovers' track leading down to Deerbolt Hall.

He remained where he was for a little while, thinking about the woman who had been Grace Ledbury and now was known as Sister Percepta. Whatever reasons had sent her to the cult of Oclixtan – personal insecurity, a search for a better understanding of life – her action had been prompted in part by the persistent importunings of her brother. But his death changed nothing for her: she was under the sway and influence of David Gilmagesh. Arnold hoped that she would find what she was seeking, but he doubted it. He had heard of too many such cults and the gullibility of their acolytes. It all tended to end in disillusion.

He made his way back down the track. There was no sign of Sister Percepta, but he caught sight of some movement at the windows of the private apartments of Deerbolt Hall. He kept his head down, making it clear he had no interest in the activities of the occupants, until he reached the area where the department intended to undertake its survey. He spent the next few hours checking the site, marking out the sections with small pegs, making notes of the possible areas for investigation – the causeway, the line of stone and ancient rubble that probably lay buried

145

under the bank, the section that he had earlier noted might be the site of a dwelling house, either an earlier part of Deerbolt Hall, or an older structure used by drovers as an inn, or a market centre. He worked on through the afternoon until the shadows began to lengthen.

From time to time during the afternoon he felt that someone was watching him but he kept working steadily. The sensation of being observed was unsettling, made him feel edgy, and from time to time he raised his head, his skin prickling, and looked about him. But there were only the trees on the hill, the silent track, and the dark stone walls of Deerbolt. The windows above him were blank, presenting a vacant face to the countryside, and he caught no glimpse of movement, yet he was constantly sensitive to the thought of watching eyes.

He was kneeling on the ground near the causeway when he finally heard the rattling of small stones. He looked up and saw Sister Simone standing at the edge of the building, staring at him. He began to rise to his feet.

'You've spent a long afternoon here,' she said. Her tone was cool, but not unsympathetic. 'And the gates of the house were barred to you when you arrived. Our hospitality is not that barren. Perhaps, when you have completed what you seek to do, you would care to come in, wash your hands, and possibly join me for some refreshment.'

Surprised, Arnold nodded. 'I'm grateful. I'm just about finished, in fact, and I hadn't intended ... I wouldn't wish to disturb you.'

A brief, thin smile appeared on her hawklike features. 'We do not find your presence disturbing, Mr Landon. We can ignore it, in the main.'

It was a neat enough put-down, he thought to himself, as she turned and disappeared around the corner of the building.

In a little while he completed what he wanted to do and walked around to his car, placed the haversack in the boot and walked into the courtyard of Deerbolt Hall. The iron-riveted gate had been opened, but he left his car outside: it was hardly worth driving it into the courtyard. A cowled woman, one of the sisters of Oclixtan, was waiting on the steps: as he drew near she turned and led the way into the room he had seen on his first arrival at

146

Deerbolt. The room was dim, heavy curtains half-drawn across the long Norman windows, and there was the now almost familiar heady, sickly-sweet scent in the air.

Sister Simone was seated there, alone. She rose, dismissed the acolyte with a murmur and then came forward, directing him. 'There is a small washroom you can use through there, Mr Landon . . .'

When he had washed his face and hands, feeling more presentable he returned to Sister Simone's presence. She acknowledged him gravely, waved him to a seat. 'So, how far have you proceeded this afternoon, Mr Landon, in these investigations of yours?'

He explained that since the visit of Gilmagesh to the Morpeth headquarters it had been decided to try to work to the Oclixtan timetable, since they did not wish to disturb the group. He told her that his work had been preliminary, but that he would be returning the following week with a group of young people who would assist in the site investigation.

'And what will that entail?'

Arnold shrugged. 'Some exploratory trenches, clearing of an area near what I believe to be an ancient causeway across a stream –'

'But the work will be finished by the end of the month?'

'It's a very tight timetable, but we hope so. Of course, it may well be we'll find something of interest which would require further investigation and then we'd ask for a further opportunity –'

'That would be impossible,' she interrupted him firmly. 'You must appreciate that we are coming to an extremely important time for Oclixtan. Our total goal is preparation for the definitive journey, that journey we must all take at the end of our lives. But for Oclixtan it will be a journey that we make voluntarily, and without relinquishing the life in our bodies, but with our senses heightened to appreciate the transcendental state we move in . . .' Her eyes seemed to glow as she spoke to him, and there was a hint of renewed passion in her voice, a deep, positive commitment that demonstrated the depth of her belief.

'We hope to finish on schedule,' he offered. 'But this journey you speak of –'

147

'David Gilmagesh has taught us that there are other, separate realms that we can travel. Your concept of space is not ours: for us, it is the otherness of the spirit realm – occupying the same space but accessible only to those of us who believe. Space for us is a means of expressing difference and separation but the journey of the shaman expresses the possibility of coming together again ... the gulf is leapt, the gulf that separates our mean, degraded existences from the divine ...'

She stopped, stared at him in silence and then said, almost accusingly, 'You met Sister Percepta on the hill.'

Surprised, Arnold nodded. 'Yes. She ... I gained the impression she was mourning her brother.'

'Mourning? No,' Sister Simone said briskly. 'She disobeyed me, walking beyond the gates, but in the circumstances ... Did you talk to her?'

'We spoke a little.'

'What did she say to you?'

There was an intense expression on the woman's hawkish features, an undercurrent of nervous suspicion in her tone. Arnold shrugged. 'We said little. I expressed my condolences, and she asked me how her brother had died. That was about all it was.'

'His death was violent, I believe,' Sister Simone said quietly. 'Did you tell her that?'

Arnold shook his head. 'I didn't want to distress her.'

'Distress ... an earthly concept she will soon leave behind, as we all will. But she should not be touching the outside world: her ordination is soon. Then, David Gilmagesh will show her the way ... The quest for grace, the crossing of the impassable gulf, only he has the skills and the courage to do this, and he will show us all the way.'

Arnold was suddenly, unreasonably irritated by her words. 'And just how does your shaman intend to do that?'

There was a short silence, and her face had darkened, anger staining her eyes. Then Sister Simone smiled grimly. Fiercely, she said, 'You do not believe, of course ... But you have *seen*, as I have seen. Oh, I know that scientific studies of shamanistic activity will try to explain away the inexplicable by psychological jargon, the language of the unbelieving scientist, talk of

148

controlled trance, maps of mental states in literal and symbolic senses. There are many who will explain . . . But the dimension of the spirits is permanently present, though it is largely hidden. The power of David Gilmagesh is that he can transcend the barriers – he can show us there is more to reality than the conscious aspect. But then, you have seen that for yourself, have you not, Mr Landon?' she added, almost sneeringly.

'I don't understand.'

'The shaman is here and he is not; he is in one reality while he also inhabits another.' Calmly, Sister Simone turned and reached across to the table beside her on which stood a silver teapot, chased with writhing serpents. 'He is a shape-shifter, as the world would say it; he can be here and not here. *As you have seen.*'

A chill seemed to touch his spine suddenly. Her eyes met his and there were deep lights there, glittering, confusing his senses. 'But you know that, Mr Landon. You have seen it. When he was not here, you saw him. You do not see him now, but he is here.'

Arnold became aware of a subtle change in the scent in the air, an odour of musk that seemed to waft gently about him. He glanced around and the light in the room seemed to have changed, dimming, blurring in an almost indefinable manner.

'He is one,' Sister Simone said softly, 'but he is also two. He is his other self. I have seen it; I have seen his power. Do you really *believe* it was David Gilmagesh you saw in the courtyard that last time you were here? His presence was required, Sister Percepta was under attack and we are but weak women, so we called, and he came . . . But had you not seen him elsewhere?' She leaned forward, dropping her voice in a conspiratorial whisper that raised the hair on the nape of his neck. 'Are you sure it was he who stood unspeaking, in front of you? I have seen him in both shapes . . . I have seen his spirit and his flesh. I have seen him as he launches himself into the cosmos and I have seen him emerge from the darkness. He can appear, Mr Landon, and he can disappear, because he has mastered the dimensions, conquered the meaning of existence, crossed the bridge between the two worlds of the body and the spirit. I have seen it . . . *we* have seen it . . .'

He was completely chilled; a coldness about his back, an icy touch at his neck. Sister Simone leaned back, picked up the silver teapot and smiled. 'Perhaps, one day, you will see it . . . again. Tea, Mr Landon?'

She began to pour the liquid into a cup. It was pale in colour, light yellow, and a pleasant, sweet odour drifted across to him. She handed him the cup. 'You will enjoy this, Mr Landon.'

'What is it?'

'I suppose you would call it . . . a form of herb tea. But new to you. Try it, Mr Landon. It will be a new experience . . .'

Detective Chief Inspector Culpeper parked his car, locked it and trudged his way up to the floor on which Arnold Landon's office was located. He glanced at his watch: he had left it somewhat late, but there was the possibility that Landon would still be working. There were still several cars in the car-park.

He climbed the stairs and walked along the corridor. Landon's office was empty. Moreover, it looked as though he might not have been there all day: a pile of files had been placed on the desk as though waiting for his attention. Culpeper hesitated, then stepped back into the corridor. He wondered whether there was anyone else around: he saw a light in the room at the end of the corridor. It was Karen Stannard's room. He tapped on the door, twisted the handle.

They were both there, Karen Stannard and her assistant, Portia Tyrrel. They were seated either side of the desk, working on some papers, minutes of a meeting, he guessed.

'Chief Inspector Culpeper! This is a surprise . . . a social call?'

Portia Tyrrel smiled at the mocking, exaggerated welcome in Karen Stannard's tone. Culpeper scowled. He never quite knew how to take the woman: she was almost too beautiful to be true, and she made him uneasy. 'I was looking for Landon.'

'Ah! Not for one of us?' she teased. 'Shame. So it'll be business. But I'm afraid he's not in the office today. Is there any way we can help?'

'I doubt it,' Culpeper growled.

'What do you want to see him about? I mean, we all work

150

together here in this department, and I know *most* of what's going on. Isn't that right, Portia?'

Portia Tyrrel made no reply, but gazed at Culpeper with an innocent air. Culpeper advanced a little further into the room. 'I'm still pursuing my enquiries into the killing of Colin Ledbury.'

'And you think Landon can help?'

'He came to see me with some information.'

Karen Stannard's eyebrows rose in feigned surprise. 'Now what on earth would Arnold know about that business in North Shields?'

Culpeper stared at her balefully. 'Nothing, it seems ... except that he was involved in some kind of fracas recently with Ledbury.'

'Fracas. Imagine that,' Karen Stannard mocked. 'He told us nothing about it, did he, Portia? But then, Arnold likes to go his own way. Fancy getting involved in a fracas. Where did this event occur, Chief Inspector?'

'At Deerbolt Hall.'

'Which is where he's working today. So was there a fight, really? And Arnold was involved? What was it about?'

Culpeper was getting vaguely annoyed at the lightness of her tone. 'It was all about Colin Ledbury trying to drag his sister Grace from Deerbolt. Apparently, she's been foolish and gullible enough to get dragged into this cult ... Oclixtan or some such rubbish ... and Landon happened to be there, got involved to some extent ...'

Portia Tyrrel frowned. 'And now Colin Ledbury's been killed. Do you think there's some connection, then?'

'Can't say, at this stage. We're following several lines of enquiry.' Briefly, his mind flitted to the task force and their hunt for the man who had arrived on Tyneside, the search for Ledbury's employee Jack Carter, and the puzzle of the death of Colonel McArdle. He thrust the thoughts aside. 'Anyway, I don't see you can help, if he's not here ...'

'One moment, Chief Inspector,' Portia Tyrrel said thoughtfully. She glanced at Karen Stannard who raised an elegant, interrogative eyebrow. 'That fax that came in this afternoon ...'

'Ah, yes ...' Karen Stannard nodded and Portia left the room to walk along the corridor. She smiled at Culpeper. 'Sit down for a moment, Chief Inspector. Portia's gone to collect something. As you know, Mr Landon has some . . . connections in the States. In fact, he's been offered a job there, though whether he'll take it or not is a moot point. Some of us hope that . . .' She hesitated, green eyes a little vague, a sudden nervousness in her slim fingers tapping on the desk. 'Well, no matter . . . The fact is, when this fax came in from the University of New Mexico, well, we are only *women* you know . . .'

She smiled conspiratorially, playing the feminine angle unsuccessfully as far as Culpeper was concerned. He knew Karen Stannard was tough, ambitious and not inclined to be ruled by feminine weaknesses.

'. . . so it was only natural that we were curious. You know, we were wondering whether Arnold had reached a decision about this job offer in the States. So Portia brought the fax to me, before she put it on his desk. But it was all rather disappointing, really . . . It didn't seem to be about the job at all. Rather, it was –'

She broke off as Portia Tyrrel entered the room, two sheets of fax paper in her hand, clipped together. Karen Stannard waved a negligent hand. 'I've explained its provenance to Chief Inspector Culpeper, Portia. But neither of us know what it's really all about.'

Culpeper took the faxed sheets and stared at them. The message had been sent from a Professor Schwartz, he noted, at the University of New Mexico Archaeological Department, and was addressed to Landon. He read it quickly, then paused. He glanced at the two women. 'This came in this afternoon? In response to some query from Landon?'

'Came in today, yes, but what questions Landon might have asked, I've no idea.' Karen Stannard leaned forward suddenly, alerted by Culpeper's manner. 'Is it important?'

'I don't know, exactly,' Culpeper replied, his mind spinning with questions. 'How did Landon come across these names?'

Silently, he read the faxed sheets again, his lips framing the names as he reached them. *Barton . . . Brazil . . . Charlie Jordan.*

He stared at the two women, his thoughts awhirl. 'Where did you say Landon had gone today?' he asked abruptly.

3

There was a sudden clattering sound, and he was aware that the cup had fallen from his hand. He stared stupidly ahead of him, and Sister Simone's face seemed to waver, dissolve into an insubstantial, drifting image.

The room seemed to grow darker and there was a high singing sound in his head. The faint light from the tall Norman windows shimmered and danced, vague wisps of grey shifting against a deep red, almost black background. His hearing was sharply enhanced, and he was surrounded by rustling sounds, the whisper of mice in corners, susurrations in the darkness, as the cowled figure in front of him shivered, twisted into smoke, faded with the scuttling whispers in the dark-cornered room.

He tried to stand but his body felt rigid, his fingers numb and his head seemed to be expanding until it was as though it filled the room. A pillar of bright light grew before his eyes, shifting in colour, performing a whirling, dazzling, dervish dance that transformed itself into layers of gleaming sky, the blush of dawn, the violent red of a blazing sunset, the purple bruised clouds of impending storm, and then all again was transmuted into a swirling expanse of the cosmos, a deep black hole within a mass of stars, a blackness into which he was hurtling with the speed of demons.

Someone was speaking to him, calling his name, but it was a name that was strangely unfamiliar and in a voice he did not recognise. The words turned to song and the singing was in his head, vague, untranslatable at first until suddenly the song took form once more, words tumbling over themselves in a river of mist. His lips formed the words but the sounds were a chant he had never heard before and the voice was not his, but a high, keening shiver ... 'Everything as it moves makes stops ... A bird as it flies stops and rests; a man when he goes forth stops when he wills; the sun is where the *oyun* and the *udaghan* have stopped, and the moon and the stars and the wind they have been with . . .'

The room was dancing, the odours in his nostrils were heavy, sensual; he heard the jagged droning of the *oyun* and was told it was the white shaman, but the song was of the *udaghan*, the female shaman, the healer, the interpreter of dreams, the foreteller of the future.

There was a vine swinging above an abyss; a slippery path between snapping, frenzied sharks; a precipitous, dizzying mountain track, the stuff of his nightmares and his fears. Wild animals were entering his body, and changing shape to spirits of the dead and he heard their speech, their dialogues with the living as they danced and twisted and intertwined their spirits with his. Voices in his head whispered of seduction and sexual blandishments, threats and warnings, power and magic and wilderness against music in a strange pentatonic scale that shimmered into his brain.

He found himself trying to cry out but his tongue was thick and his nerve centres deadened. He had lost control of his limbs and yet he was floating in the mist river, rising above the earth, traversing vast forests, drifting along a pathway that was air, and fog and water, insubstantial, shivering, the pathway of ancient ancestors under a sky of blood . . .

He stood up, but his senses were swimming and in his visions he crossed bleak, lifeless steppes towards a dark iron mountain against which the sky seemed to thunder and clash with brilliant flashes of light, but against it he heard a long wailing sound, the cry of the eagle . . . *'We have been waiting for you. We knew you would come. You will have a ghost with you always, your other self . . .'* and the vision shimmered and broke and he knew the universe, the cosmic tree as his soul was kidnapped by the snarling jaguar. It called him from the deep forest, it came screaming and it carried him to the black and yellow orchid that lay wind-ridden at the centre of the universe.

He tried to move, walk forward to escape his dreams, and he became aware of a crashing sound; it faded into the light tinkling of bells and in a brief flash of light he saw someone standing beside him. A dark cowl, and then another, insubstantial figure moving swiftly towards him, black and vague in outline but

154

powerful, angry, vicious words spitting from its mouth. The words roared into his consciousness ... *Stupidity, stupidity ...* but they faded and whispered and there was a long silence as his brain twisted and danced and shuddered in an uncontrolled frenzy.

There was a hand on his shoulder, a face, dark-visaged, close to his; the smile was powerful and the hand that gripped his was reassuring, until it began spinning him around, whirling him in a painted dance of yellows, and reds and blues. Panic rose in his throat as he saw the image of David Gilmagesh rise up with him in the dance but there were two images: one a horned figure soaring to the sky world, and he heard the rattling of the gourds that contained the seeds, the pebbles, the souls and spirits of his ancestors. The dance stopped abruptly and he had the sensation of falling, a deep plunging down through shifting fronds of green weed, past dark, gem-encrusted rocks, down into darkness and the shimmering floor of the ocean. The swirling dim world he inhabited now was peaceful, but there was a new imperative and the climb back was long, a clambering up a twisted thread to the sky where the spirits danced and sang.

Stupidity ... stupidity ...

It was as though a curtain of mist had parted momentarily allowing him to see. There was a cool breeze on his face and he was walking. Above him the sky was pale, but shot with brief flashes of light and he stumbled until a gentle hand touched his, leading him forward, rising, climbing until the breath was harsh in his chest as he reeled, struggling to find his footsteps, his legs leaden, his senses numbed.

He felt himself stumbling and he shook his dizzied head. He realised he was really out in the open air, someone beside him, guiding him, and he saw trees, a pathway; but a moment later a distant, growing, glowing ball of fire hurtled towards him, engulfed him in its light but he was not burned, even though the breath in his chest was hot and painful. He knew he was staggering as though intoxicated; his legs ached as though he were climbing a long, steep hill and he fell, aware of gravel and stone scarring his hands. But his senses reeled again, the shimmering figure ahead of him beckoned and he followed in his journey to the stars.

155

His whole body was shuddering, but it was as though he were in a tunnel, his attention focused on the silent, slowly moving figure ahead of him, calling him on, while around him there was a reduced awareness, unfocused glimpses of movement, of solidity, of trees and darkening sky.

There was another sudden burst of clarity, a shattering ecstasy, and he saw the hill, smelt the woods, knew his name again and cried out, but the figure ahead of him was capering, whispering, calling and the curtains of mist descended once more, a mist that turned red and impenetrable. The music that gripped him was wild, an ecstasy of power, and once more he heard the cry of the eagle, his other self, his existence in the spirit world.

He climbed, plundering the heights; he climbed, riding the winds; his mind told him there were dizzying precipices to conquer, and clashing rocks to evade. He descended into the jaws of the earth, and a long, slow-moving green sea of rank weed opened up in front of him, but he sailed it on a membrane of ice; he gripped tendrils of smoke to haul himself forward across an ancient bridge, thin as a hair, that led onwards, while below him the bones of those who had fallen gleamed palely in the gloomy depths of the chasm. But then he became suddenly, blindingly aware once more that he was staggering through trees and was out on the rocky hill, in the open air, where the land fell away in long, undulating folds and the faint light of a dying sun illuminated his hands held out in front of him, shaking, ethereal in their paleness.

His hands. They were reality.

He saw them, was aware of the cold, shivering reality of his flesh, and he realised too that he was sweating, his body shaking with bouts of cold, ice in his veins, and yet a hot thudding, drumming of blood in his head. He closed his eyes, shut his lids tightly, and when he opened them again he saw the land and the faded, bruised clouds were still there ahead of him. There was a sickness in his throat, and his body was shuddering violently, but the visions were now less powerful, their effect less shattering, the clashing colours had gone from his mind and he heard the faint whisper of a breeze, felt its light touch on his cheek. He looked down. Blackness yawned in front of him and he leaned, stooped forward, almost falling outward into its depths.

He was on the hill. He was standing at the edge of the quarry on the hill above Deerbolt Hall. There was an incoherence in his mind, a struggling as he forced himself to thrust reality back into his brain, retain its impact, overcome the intrusion of other sounds, lights that beckoned him, voices that whispered insanity in his ears. He dropped to his knees and harsh stone cut him: the physical pain helped thrust back the visions, and he looked about him again, concentrating on the dark blue of the hills in the distance, feeling the wind in his face, fighting down the sickness that still threatened to rise and choke him. The empty fall of the quarry still lay before him, opening out as though to embrace him. Then the old, almost superstitious feeling that he was being watched came over him again and he looked back over his shoulder.

He was not alone, in the woods above the quarry edge. For a long moment there was nothing to be seen. Then slowly, as though emerging from a dark mist he saw a man. His clothes were dark, his features indistinguishable at first and his image seemed to shimmer and dance, sway to some unheard song. Then he began to walk forward, come closer and there was a name . . .

Landon . . .

The tunnel was widening; his focus was clearing; his peripheral vision was returning and he struggled to his feet. The man coming towards him seemed to be rushing, and yet barely moved, his progress agonisingly slow, stately. His hands were outstretched, the fingers long and crooked, the blond hair of his head flying in the wind, and Landon knew he was death.

He dropped to his knees, involuntarily, and the shaman seemed to float towards him, reaching for his shoulders, and there was one long moment when it was almost as though they were clasping each other as lovers. He felt a violent push against his upper chest, a shoving backwards towards emptiness, but instincts of self-preservation rushed through him, taking control, and his hands gripped the dark cloth in front of him in fierce desperation. There was a stamping and surging but his grip was inexorable, powered by sudden panic, and for a long moment it was as though they were poised, motionless, balanced on the

157

edge of eternity. Next moment they were both launched into the void.

He felt himself falling, twisting in the air, and it was like the earlier journeys he had experienced, an endless dream, but now more real. The fall seemed endless, a rushing of wind in his ears and yet it was only a moment. Then there was the thudding, shuddering pain in his back, his left shoulder crashing into a rocky outcrop; the pressure on his neck and upper body was suddenly released and he saw the shaman fly, disappearing into the blackness with a long, wailing cry that seemed to fill the sky endlessly, until it was cut off abruptly and a long slow silence crept up to the ledge on which he lay. He stayed there motionless, half-stunned, until slowly the feeling came back into his limbs. He felt the coldness of rock against his face and he shivered; but as his sense of feeling returned to him so there was a black mist slowly falling over his brain, until at last there was a drifting, a silence, and peace, and a vast nothingness . . .

He had no idea how long he lay there. It was dark when he woke. His tongue was thick and furred; his headache was violent, a throbbing, thundering sound in his temples. Cautiously, he raised himself on one elbow. In the dim light he could see that he was lying on some kind of ledge; above him, silhouetted against the faint light of the sky, he could make out the outline of the quarry rim. He lay there, unable to move for a while, and gradually it all came back to him, the whirling dreams, the man up here with him on the hill. The struggle.

He turned his head carefully, peered over the edge to look down into the quarry. There was nothing to be seen, but down there, he guessed, would lie the body of the shaman, the shape-shifter, David Gilmagesh.

He closed his eyes, unable to comprehend the reasons that lay behind the action of Sister Simone in drugging him, the attack by the shaman, and then he became aware there were lights dancing in the sky above the quarry edge. He tried to call out, but there was only a croaking sound. He heard his name called, and again he tried to respond. Then the lights were flashing in his eyes, and there were sounds of reassurance. He lay back and waited, and in a while he heard someone scrambling down on a rope. A harness was strapped around him and he was lifted out

158

of the chasm and he recalled the wild flight he had taken with the shaman, with its colours, and its dreams and its violent, hallucinogenic visions of the cosmos . . .

Surprisingly, after a little while he was able to walk. There was no medical team with the men who had hauled him from the quarry: he recognised Culpeper, but the other policemen were strangers. In a little while they made their way back down the hill, Arnold half-supported by a young policeman's arm, and they came down to Deerbolt Hall, and made their way back into the reception room he seemed to have left so long ago.

'You'd better wait here until we sort a few things out. You're in no condition to drive. I've called an ambulance and I'll get one of the lads to follow in your car.'

Arnold nodded to Culpeper, and gratefully took the seat offered him. After a while he raised his head and looked around at the other people who were in the room. He saw Sister Percepta first, talking to Culpeper and a sergeant Arnold did not recognise: the man was taking notes, the woman's head was held low. She seemed uneasy, and tearful. He looked around and saw Sister Simone sitting in the corner. Her back was stiff, and she glared straight ahead of her. Her mouth was set grimly, and she paid no attention to Arnold. It was though she refused to recognise the presence of the man she had prepared for death.

Arnold's glance slipped past her to the man standing against the wall. For several moments he failed to recognise him, and then slowly his mind took in the dark clothing, the lean face . . . but he was different in some indescribable way, his hair darker, or perhaps it was a trick of the light. But then he knew. He knew, and yet it could not be possible. The man he saw lay in the quarry, he could not have survived the fall, and yet . . .

'Gilmagesh!'

The man's eyes flickered towards Arnold momentarily, then turned away. He made no response. Culpeper heard Arnold cry out however, and looked around. He stared at the man against the wall for a few moments and then he looked at Arnold, shaking his head.

'No, that's not David Gilmagesh. His name is Timothy Brazil.'

4

There was an air of clear hostility as they sat silently, waiting. When the Chief Constable finally entered the conference room they all rose: Culpeper, O'Connor, Farnsby and Garcia. The Chief Constable took his seat at the head of the table and gestured to the others to sit down. He was silent for a little while, shuffling papers in front of him, and then he said, 'I've seen the report of the preliminary interview with this man Jack Carter. It would seem that he corroborates most of what you've reported to me, Chief Inspector Culpeper.' His cold glance rose, fixed on Culpeper's face. 'Since you seem to have pieced it all together now, perhaps you'd better enlighten the rest of the group here.'

'If that's what you wish, sir,' Culpeper said cheerfully. He looked around at his colleagues: they had a generally crestfallen air, only Farnsby looking in the least mutinous, but then, he would be enjoying Culpeper's triumph least of all. 'As you say, I think I've got most of it, though some of it we've yet to prove conclusively . . . But the plain fact is, the task force were looking for the wrong man, all the time.'

Clearly irritated, O'Connor leaned forward. 'Not the wrong man, exactly,' he countered bleakly. 'We just pinned the wrong identity on him. The man we were looking for certainly did set up a new distribution ring on Tyneside – it's just that we got his name wrong.'

'As you got the identity of the man fished out of the sea wrong,' Culpeper reminded him.

Inspector Raoul Garcia could not let that pass. He let out a small, explosive sound from between his teeth, and shrugged expressive Spanish shoulders. 'The initial identification was difficult. We made a reasonable supposition, backed by information from Barcelona –'

'Which had been deliberately laid, planted by Brazil before he fled to Newcastle,' Culpeper interrupted happily. 'He'd put the body belt on the corpse, and then he went back to Barcelona to leave other pointers, so that you'd think it was Charlie Jordan making the trip to Newcastle.'

'It's easy to be smug with hindsight. Sir.' Farnsby said, nettled at Culpeper's triumphalism. 'Particularly when in the end it was all a matter of luck, and being in the right place at the right time. If it hadn't been for the information sent to Landon from the States –'

'But it was *I* who was there to receive it,' Culpeper reminded him, magnanimous enough to overlook Farnsby's sharpness, but determined to rub home the point.

'Gentlemen, this is a debriefing,' the Chief Constable said sourly. 'No need to scratch at old sores. Culpeper, you'd better give the group the gist of what's in your report to me. And it would help if you made it somewhat chrononological . . .'

'I'm happy to do that, sir,' Culpeper said, and was. 'Though Inspector Farnsby is quite right in saying it fell together only when Professor Schwartz faxed some information to Arnold Landon.' He paused, enjoying the moment. 'Schwartz had a contact in the IRS in the States, and when he made enquiries, at Landon's request it would seem, he received rather more information than he had requested. He discovered that the man Landon was asking about – Barton – had not only been using a pseudonym when he was in the Mojave desert, but that he was actually one of twins. His real name was David Brazil, and his brother, his more or less identical twin, was Timothy James Brazil. The man Inspectors Garcia and O'Connor thought had been murdered.'

There was a short, uneasy silence. O'Connor's saturnine features were wooden. Culpeper smiled and continued. 'In fact, the man chewed up by the fishing vessel propellers was not Timothy Brazil – it was his brother David Brazil's accomplice in the States, Charlie Jordan. And that's where we should start, I suppose. In the States, I mean.'

'If it keeps things simple,' the Chief Constable agreed drily.

Culpeper nodded, and beamed around the room. 'The two brothers had gone their own ways some ten years ago – they had a predilection towards criminal activity, though Tim Brazil was always rather more . . . vicious. David Brazil thought himself more intellectual, and was into scams. He tried various con tricks but had a flair for the mystical and ended up founding a cult, moving about, gulling vulnerable people out of their money. He saw an opportunity in the Mojave desert, which is where Professor Schwartz came across him, practising his cult based on shamanism. David Brazil – who at that time called himself Barton – was supported in this by a small-time crook called Charlie Jordan. It's not quite clear what problem arose between them, but their relationship had become an uneasy one. Jordan felt he was being sidelined, thought he deserved a bigger cut of profits, and there was bad blood between him and David Brazil. Anyway, the roof fell in on both of them when they were investigated by the Inland Revenue Service, so they decided to get out of the States. They came to Europe. They came looking for David's brother, Timothy. Who by then was heavily involved in the drug scene in Barcelona.'

'Where he had developed sticky fingers, and was robbing his own accomplices,' Garcia intervened, unwilling to be left out of the account.

Culpeper glared at him. This was *his* story. 'It seems David Brazil wanted to get rid of Charlie Jordan, who was becoming a liability, redundant to Brazil's plans, yet battening on what Brazil saw as his scams – shamanism – and doing little for his cut of the proceeds. And besides, meeting up with his brother after all these years, and realising Tim Brazil was in trouble, gave him an idea. His shaman scam included the claim that he could shape-shift, have another self – if his brother came in with him, they could develop what became the Oclixtan cult into a money-spinner. They could stand in for each other at appropriate times, practise their trickery more easily with two people involved, gull the rich, vulnerable women all the more effectively. With the assistance of their hallucinogenic drugs they could even persuade them there were *two* David Brazils.'

'It could also help provide an alibi occasionally,' Farnsby growled.

Culpeper could afford to ignore him. 'But though Tim Brazil saw this as a way out of his difficulties in Spain, he was unwilling to give up his own activity entirely. A new identity, merging with his brother, was an attractive proposition. But first, Timothy

Brazil to all intents and purposes had to disappear. Or better still ... die.'

O'Connor shifted in his seat, and stared at his hands. Defensively, he said, 'The body we dragged out of the sea could have been anyone. There were no real distinguishing marks, Forensic couldn't help us, and it was reasonable to suppose it was –'

'Timothy Brazil. Quite.' Culpeper smiled and nodded. 'But it wasn't. The Brazil brothers took the now redundant Charlie Jordan on board the *Dawn Princess*, killed him, dumped him overboard and then presumably scuttled the yacht. Tim Brazil went back to Barcelona, laid a few convincing clues behind, assumed Jordan's name and flew to Newcastle, where he promptly vanished.'

'To Deerbolt Hall,' Farnsby muttered.

'Joining his brother,' Culpeper agreed. 'And there it was all set up: the Oclixtan cult had already drawn in a number of gullible women who had brought quite large sums of money into the grasp of David Gilmagesh – as David Brazil now called himself – and there was Timothy to put in the occasional bewildering appearance as his other self. We've had a closer look at the Hall now: there's quite an intricate series of tricks there – dimming lights, most rooms bugged with controls in the private apartments, incense – all the systems that could be used to create an illusion of shape-shifting, and mystery, and flight through the use of drugs ... not least the hallucinogenic substance known as peyote ...'

The Chief Constable nodded. 'Jack Carter's statement admits that he knew Timothy Brazil had entered the Tyneside distribution network, though he knew him as Jordan. It was only when he saw him in the courtyard at Deerbolt –'

'I was coming to that, sir,' Culpeper interrupted, unwilling to be overridden in his moment of triumph. 'Yes, they broadened the base of the cult, but Timothy Brazil stuck to his old ways in addition, and got involved in the drugs distribution business along the river. In between times he stayed at Deerbolt, and played his part in the charade. But he became concerned when he realised they were being watched. Colonel McArdle was up there, regularly on the hill with binoculars with an agenda of his own. David Gilmagesh wasn't too much concerned, but his brother Timothy came from a tougher background. He thought their situation might be exposed, the fact that there were really two of them. So he arranged for the introduction of a drug into McArdle's system, and persuaded the colonel he could fly. From the bell tower of his manor house.'

'Bad mistake, really,' O'Connor muttered. 'Drawing attention to themselves . . .'

'Maybe, maybe,' Culpeper conceded magnanimously, 'but then, your task force was never interested in the McArdle case, was it?'

O'Connor bridled at the veiled criticism. 'There was no clear connection –'

'*Gentlemen*,' the Chief Constable warned.

Culpeper beamed, and returned to his leading role. 'Anyway, it wasn't too long before another complication loomed. Colin Ledbury was anxious to persuade his sister to allow him to put money into a building development consortium, but under his pressure she disappeared. Not too far up the road, as it happened – just to Oclixtan – but he chased around looking for her for some time.'

'Which *you* did not,' the Chief Constable said sourly.

Culpeper loftily ignored the criticism. 'He finally traced her to Deerbolt Hall, went there, tried to make her see sense, ended up attempting to drag her away . . . and that's when Timothy Brazil turned up, returning from Newcastle. We have Arnold Landon's account of the incident. It seems that David Gilmagesh was actually at the house, holed up in the private apartments, keeping out of the way, but his brother rolled up in the middle of the altercation, and Jack Carter, with his own drug connections on Tyneside, recognised him. He knew him as Charlie Jordan, of course, but he also knew the man was dangerous so he pulled Ledbury away. As for Ledbury's death thereafter, well, it's only supposition so far, but –'

'Carter's statement seems to confirm your suppositions, Culpeper,' the Chief Constable announced reluctantly. 'Carter was apprehended in Manchester, trying to take a plane out to Amsterdam, but we managed to get him –'

'With some assistance and information from Interpol,' Inspector Garcia said brightly.

164

'Yes,' Culpeper admitted but with some doubt in his voice. 'Our guess, now supported by Carter, was that Carter told Ledbury who the man in the courtyard was and Ledbury was stupid enough to seek him out at Shields, approach him to help get Grace Ledbury out of Oclixtan . . . but Timothy Brazil merely saw the approach as another danger, a possible exposure of his real identity. He solved the problem in his usual way. With violence. He put a knife in Ledbury's ribs –'

'Stomach,' O'Connor contradicted.

'He killed him,' Culpeper said, glaring at the man from York.

'So now Timothy Brazil can be charged with the murders of Charlie Jordan, Colonel McArdle and Colin Ledbury, and the attempted murder of Arnold Landon,' Inspector Farnsby suggested.

Culpeper regarded the younger man with a certain satisfaction. 'Well, no, that's not exactly right. It's pretty clear that David Gilmagesh and Timothy Brazil knocked off Charlie Jordan and dumped him off the *Dawn Princess*. They were both in on that killing. Brazil was always the more violent brother – and he took matters into his own hands, with the killing of both the colonel and Colin Ledbury. So it seems Gilmagesh wasn't involved in those murders, he was even annoyed because he saw the obvious dangers in the death of McArdle and Ledbury. The trail could lead, as it did, to Deerbolt Hall.'

'But the attempt on Landon . . .'

'Ah, now, that was a rather different kettle of fish . . .'

Karen Stannard crossed her legs. They were sheathed in smooth nylon; elegant in shape, they drew Arnold's glance as she knew they would. Arnold looked away after a moment, annoyed with himself, and Karen smiled in Portia Tyrrel's direction, as though she had won some minor victory. 'So what's going to happen to Oclixtan now?' she asked.

Arnold shrugged. 'It's finished, of course. David Gilmagesh dead in the quarry; his brother in jail and charged with murder. The cult is finished. The Hall will be up for sale. I suppose the proceeds will be used to help pay for Timothy Brazil's defence.'

'Will not those women – the sisters of Oclixtan – recover the assets they handed over to Gilmagesh?' Portia asked.

'I understand Grace Ledbury may well recover what *she'd* put in, because there hadn't been time to convert it, but for the rest of the twelve women, it's a bit uncertain. They gave it freely in the first instance, of course, and much of it was spent, some squirrelled away in various bank accounts, some of it used to fund Timothy Brazil's drug dealing . . . it's all rather complicated.'

'And Sister Simone?' Karen Stannard asked.

'As far as I understand from Chief Inspector Culpeper,' Arnold replied carefully, 'she'll be treated as an accessory, and as a major prosecution witness. There's some doubt about just what she knew, though both he and I believe she knew more than she's letting on. She was committed to David Gilmagesh, probably almost convinced about his powers, though she must have known about the existence of his twin brother. What we do know is that she was certainly involved in the death of Colonel McArdle.'

'In what way?'

'Timothy Brazil persuaded her to go to see the colonel at Riggs Manor. McArdle was always a ladies' man, and was also keen to settle the business about the building work at Deerbolt. He would have welcomed Sister Simone around for a drink. Culpeper reckons that she's insisting she was put up to it by Brazil, who persuaded her to slip some peyote into a drink she had with the colonel. But she then says she left . . . it was Brazil who sneaked in later and led McArdle up to the bell tower.'

Portia Tyrrel frowned. 'And presumably pushed him over. But was it Timothy Brazil who also put her up to drugging you in the same way?'

Arnold recalled the image of Sister Simone, smiling, offering him the cup of what she described as herb tea . . . 'It seems not. He denies it, anyway. No, she'd done it in respect of McArdle, to assist Timothy Brazil – though she still claims she thought it was the shaman – but drugging me was apparently her own idea. It had worked with McArdle, and as a committed believer in

Oclixtan and David Gilmagesh, she thought I posed a similar danger as McArdle, snooping around the Hall, staring up at the windows ... So she drugged me, and then called Gilmagesh, expecting to be praised for her commitment.'

'And?' Karen Stannard asked, leaning forward so that the blouse fell open at her throat, exposing the tanned skin, the first swell of her breasts. Doggedly, Arnold ignored the vision.

'To her surprise he was furious. I know ... when I was reeling under the drug, I heard someone shouting about stupidity ...'

'But it *was* Gilmagesh who led you up to the quarry,' Portia Tyrrel objected quietly.

Arnold shrugged. 'That's right. I think by then he felt trapped. He was not inclined to the same violence as his brother but he now felt he had to take the same way out of a difficulty, do as his brother had done with McArdle. Sister Simone's actions had left him no choice, but he was furious, because he knew it was crazy, dangerous ...'

'And he fell to his death.'

The room was silent for a little while. Arnold thought back to the whirling colours in his brain, the dances, the sounds, the brilliant images that had exploded inside his head, until his mind began to clear in those final minutes, when the effects of the peyote had begun to wear off. It was then that David Gilmagesh had tried to force him over the edge of the quarry and had ended by hurtling to his death himself.

'Do you think you would have got out of the quarry by yourself?' Karen Stannard asked curiously.

Arnold shook his head. 'I don't know. I was weak ... I think it was just as well that Sister Percepta had seen Gilmagesh leading me up the hill, towards the quarry where she had seen me earlier. So when Culpeper arrived, leading the cavalry charge ...'

'And for that you can thank Miss Tyrrel here,' Karen Stannard purred. 'Although she should not, of course, have looked at a private fax intended for your own eyes. Still, if she hadn't read it, and hadn't shown it to Culpeper, you could have been on that ledge even now.'

Portia Tyrell's features displayed no emotion, but her eyes dwelt cynically on Karen Stannard for a few moments before she turned back to Arnold. 'When *we* looked at the fax *we* didn't understand it, of course. It was all about the Mojave cult, a man called Barton whose real name was David Brazil; the fact that the IRS had traced his records to show that he was a twin; that some man called Jordan had left the States with him . . . It was all very mysterious as far as we were concerned.'

'Portia looked at it because she thought it might be something to do with your intentions with regard to the job offer from the University of New Mexico,' Karen Stannard said, smiling brilliantly. 'However, it made no reference to that. But . . . perhaps you've had other correspondence regarding that matter.'

There had been other correspondence, but Arnold was disinclined to discuss it with Karen or Portia. It was none of their business. But it had enabled him to make up his mind regarding the offer from Professor Schwartz. He raised his head, looked Karen directly in the eyes. They were green in colour, unfathomable as usual.

'I've decided to reject Don Schwartz's offer. I won't be going to the States.'

Karen said nothing for a little while, but there was a subtle change in her eyes. The colour seemed to become softer, more indeterminate, as she held his glance: he felt there was a conflict of emotions behind those eyes, an uncertainty that left her out of control for a moment, and there was a subtle change in her breathing. Her left hand crept up to the neck of her blouse, eased it higher, drawing it together, her fingers lightly brushing her throat. Then she looked away. Arnold glanced across to Portia: she was watching Karen with a certain interest.

'So,' Karen breathed at last, 'not even the combined efforts of the Brazils, Sister Simone and Professor Don Schwartz can accomplish your removal from the Department of Museums and Antiquities.'

'It seems so,' he replied. 'You're stuck with me, looks like.'

There was something in the remark which appeared to amuse Portia Tyrrel.

Back in his office Arnold looked again at the letter from Jane Wilson. It bore the postmark of the university, in New Mexico. It was a friendly letter, although a little sad in places, but it was firm in its decisions, and logical in its argument. He read the final sentences again.

'You'll be aware that I've felt for some time that we were drifting apart. The job offer Don made you, had you accepted it, would have probably secured our future together. But your delay in replying can really mean only one thing, to me, and to us I suppose. Don made you an offer – but I know you'll never take it up. He's also made me an offer. It's one, in the circumstances, I think I'm going to accept . . .'

He sat staring out of the window for a little while. She was right. Don Schwartz had asked her to marry him, and it made sense for her to accept. The gulf that had lain between Arnold and Jane Wilson had become one not only of time and space, but also of understanding . . . He and Jane had been friends, and lovers, for some time. But somehow he had been unable to show her the commitment she desired.

It had perhaps been inevitable. It was over. He wished them well.

As for himself . . . there were files on his desk and the obsession which seemed to rule his life. Old stones, ancient timber, the detritus of the past . . .

He suddenly became aware of the slim figure of Portia Tyrrel, standing in the doorway. She was watching him with wise eyes, a slight smile on her lips. 'Are you all right, Arnold?'

He nodded. 'Of course.'

'All settled, then.'

'So it seems.'

She watched him silently as he folded the letter between his fingers and slipped it into his wallet. 'I'm glad you're not leaving the department,' she said. She hesitated, then added, 'And so is *she*, you know. Though I suspect maybe she'll never tell you . . .'